THE JUPITER PIRATES

BOOK 1: HUNT FOR THE *HYDRA*

· BOOK ONE ·

THE JUPITER PIRATES

HUNT FOR THE HYDRA

BY JASON FRY

HARPER

An Imprint of HarperCollinsPublishers

Library of Congress Cataloging-in-Publication Data
Fry, Jason, 1969–
   Hunt for the Hydra / by Jason Fry. — First edition.
      pages   cm — (The Jupiter pirates ; book 1)
   Summary: "A family of space privateers becomes embroiled in a
solar system-wide conspiracy, all while the three siblings compete to
determine who will become the next captain of the ship when their
mother steps down"— Provided by publisher.
   ISBN 978-0-06-223020-1 (hardback)
   [1. Science fiction. 2. Space ships—Fiction. 3. Pirates—Fiction.
4. Conspiracies—Fiction. 5. Brothers and sisters—Fiction.] I. Title.
PZ7.F9224Hu 2014   2013032154
[Fic]—dc23   CIP
                                                              AC

Typography by Anna Christian
❖
13 14 15 16 17   CG/RRDH   10 9 8 7 6 5 4 3 2 1
First Edition

FOR EMILY AND JOSHUA,

THE BEST CREW ANY

PIRATE COULD IMAGINE

911
AGAMEMNON

1172
AENEAS

EARTH

624
HEKTOR

HIGH PORT

GANYMEDE

INHABITED MOONS AND ASTERIODS OF

JUPITER

PORT TOWN

CALLISTO

IO

GALILEO STATION

JUPITER

617
PATROCLUS

PROTECTORATE
OF EUROPA

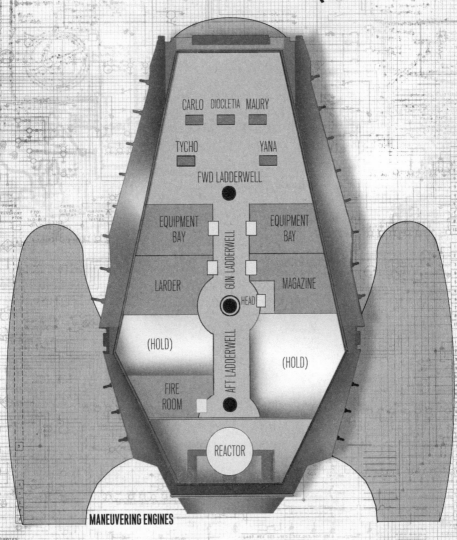

THE SHADOW COMET

QUARTER DECK

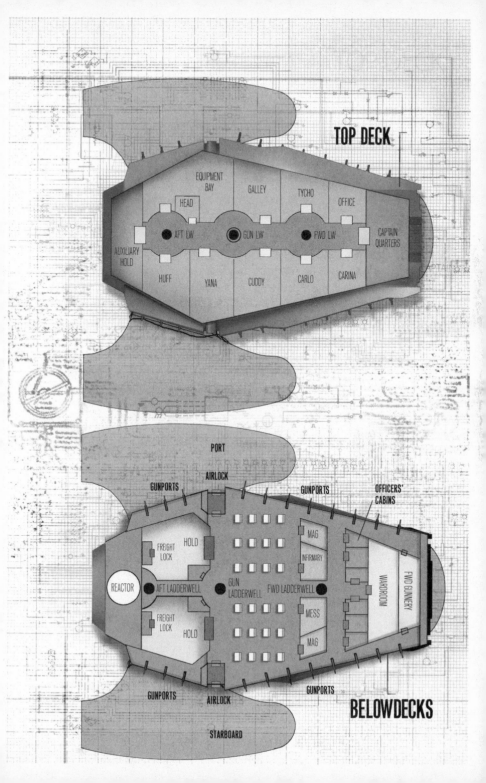

TOP DECK

EQUIPMENT BAY

HEAD

GALLEY

TYCHO

OFFICE

AFT LW

GUN LW

FWD LW

CAPTAIN QUARTERS

AUXILIARY HOLD

HUFF

YANA

CUDDY

CARLO

CARINA

PORT

AIRLOCK

GUNPORTS

GUNPORTS

OFFICERS' CABINS

FREIGHT LOCK

HOLD

MAG

INFIRMARY

REACTOR

AFT LADDERWELL

GUN LADDERWELL

FWD LADDERWELL

WARDROOM

FWD GUNNERY

FREIGHT LOCK

HOLD

MESS

MAG

GUNPORTS

AIRLOCK

GUNPORTS

STARBOARD

BELOWDECKS

CONTENTS

1

DEEP SPACE ENCOUNTER

Tycho Hashoone was doing his math homework when the alarms started shrieking.

For a moment, Tycho was confused. The quarter-deck of the *Shadow Comet* was dark, and the rest of the bridge crew had retired to their cabins hours ago. The only light came from the white square of Tycho's computer monitor and the readouts on the other crew consoles. Outside the viewports lay deep space, filled with stars like spilled jewels.

A moment before, all had been quiet except for the hum of the *Comet*'s atmosphere pumps. Now, it was *loud*.

"Knock it off, Vesuvia!" Tycho yelled, his hands shaky with adrenaline. "I'm awake! I was awake before! What's going on?"

"Long-range sensors indicate a single object," said the cool, flat voice of Vesuvia, the software program that the *Comet*'s computer brain used to communicate with her crew. "Length of object estimated at approximately two hundred meters. Distance to object approximately fifteen thousand kilometers and closing."

"Great," Tycho said. "Turn off that stupid alarm before I go deaf. And get these math problems off my screen."

"You have not completed your homework assignment," Vesuvia objected. "Your mother will not approve."

"Come on, Vesuvia—I'm not going to complete it during an intercept," Tycho said, sighing in exasperation. It was true that he was only twelve, but he *was* the watch officer.

"Acknowledged," Vesuvia said. The alarms stopped wailing and the math problems disappeared. "Awaiting orders."

Breathe, Tycho reminded himself. *Think! You've done two intercepts already and been through this drill hundreds of times.*

"Put the tactical readout on the main screen," Tycho said. "Send all sensor data to my monitor. And bring up the lights."

"Acknowledged," Vesuvia said.

Tycho blinked at the sudden brightness of the quarter-deck lights. On the main screen, a cross marked where the *Comet* lay in wait behind a thin screen of dust and debris that had once been an asteroid. On the other side of the map, a flashing triangle showed the mysterious object's location. A dotted line showed that if the object kept to its current course, it would pass very close to where the *Comet* was hidden.

"Shall I charge up the engines and guns?" Vesuvia asked.

"Let's wait until we know what we've got," Tycho said, feeling calmer now. "But give me full power on all sensor masts and scanning antennas."

"The plural of 'antenna' is 'antennae,'" Vesuvia corrected him. "Order acknowledged."

Tycho heard a faint hum as the *Comet* extended her sensor arms into the vacuum of space, scanning the approaching object.

"Ion emissions detected," Vesuvia said. "Calculating profile."

Tycho grinned. Ion emissions meant the object had a power source attached to it. It wasn't some rogue asteroid tumbling through the vast darkness of the solar system—it was a ship. But what kind of ship? And more importantly, what was her allegiance?

That question made Tycho stop grinning. If the approaching ship turned out to be an Earth warship, the *Comet* would have to make a run for it. Most Earth warships were bigger and better armed than the *Comet*, and all of them treated privateers as enemy vessels.

"Now you can charge the engines and guns," Tycho told Vesuvia. "And where's that sensor profile?"

"Still calculating," Vesuvia said.

Tycho drummed his fingers on the surface of his console, reminding himself to be patient.

"Calculations complete," Vesuvia announced. "Profile fits Orion-class bulk freighter attached to long-range fuel tanks. Ninety-seven point six two percent match to factory model."

"Yes!" Tycho exulted.

Freighters carried cargoes—sometimes valuable ones—and privateers like the Hashoones made their living by seizing those cargoes.

As Tycho's mother, Diocletia, never failed to point out, privateers weren't the same as pirates. Pirates ignored the law, preying on any spacecraft that had the misfortune to stray into their gunsights. They stole cargoes and mistreated the ships' crews they imprisoned—if they didn't sell them into slavery or kill them.

Privateers conducted themselves differently. They obeyed the laws of space, kept careful records about the cargoes they seized, treated prisoners well, and released them as soon as possible. And they used force only when necessary. Those rules were part of the Hashoones' letter of marque, the document that authorized them to attack enemy ships on behalf of their home government, the Jovian Union, composed of the nearly two dozen inhabited moons of Jupiter, Saturn, and Uranus.

The sensor profile strongly suggested the ship out there was just a big, lumbering freighter—but whose freighter? If she was Jovian, Tycho would have to let her pass. If she flew the flag of Earth . . .

"Hail the bridge crew!" he ordered Vesuvia. "And beat to quarters!"

Tycho heard the bridge crew before he saw them—their footsteps echoed as they descended the forward ladderwell connecting the quarterdeck with the top deck above, which housed his family's living quarters. From belowdecks, meanwhile, came the urgent call of pipes as the bosun played the tune ordering the *Comet*'s crewers to lash up and stow their hammocks. Tycho could hear the leaders of the gunnery crews barking orders, preparing to fling open the *Comet*'s gunports and winch the barrels of her weapons out through the hull. The crewers not assigned to the guns would be strapping on pistols and swords, singing and boasting about what they would do with their shares of the prize money from a freighter full of rich goods.

Tycho's older brother, sixteen-year-old Carlo, was the first of the bridge crew to arrive. He rubbed sleep from his dark brown eyes.

Carlo grunted at Tycho and buckled himself into his own chair on the port side of the quarterdeck, just forward of Tycho's console. He jabbed at switches, bringing his instruments to life. With a whine, a U-shaped control yoke rose from beneath Carlo's console. His hands closed around it and Tycho saw him stretch slightly, feet finding the familiar pedals.

"Vesuvia, test pilot controls," Carlo said with a yawn.

"Acknowledged," Vesuvia said.

Carlo manipulated the control yoke with a practiced hand. The *Shadow Comet*'s systems could be operated from any of the stations of her quarterdeck—each station had its own yoke and pedals that could be used for steering. But Carlo's station traditionally belonged to the *Comet*'s pilot, just as Tycho's was normally used for communications and navigation.

"Controls feel good, Vesuvia," Carlo said, yawning again. "What's going on, little brother?"

Carlo was an expert pilot, with a natural feel for the *Comet*'s controls. Tycho knew it would be wise to let him steer the ship. But Tycho was the current watch officer, so that was his decision—and he didn't like that his brother simply assumed he'd take over the piloting.

"Looks like an Orion," Tycho said. "She's eleven thousand klicks out."

Carlo instantly looked more awake. "Whose flag is she flying?" he asked.

"No response to transponder queries," Tycho said. "She's probably trying to figure out who we are."

That wasn't a surprise. Unless they were traveling very close to home, freighters and civilian starships rarely used transponders to automatically identify themselves and where they came from—that would just make the job of pirates and privateers easier. Tycho and Carlo knew the freighter's crew must be frantically scanning the area ahead, trying to figure out what kind of ship was lying in wait for them and whose flag she was flying.

The *Comet*'s bells began to *clang-clang*, as they did every half hour. Five bells meant it was 0230.

A thud marked the arrival of Tycho's twin sister, Yana, who'd grabbed the outsides of the ladder and dropped onto the quarterdeck without bothering to put her feet on the rungs.

"This better be good, Tycho. I was having the *best* dream," Yana said.

"Is an Orion good enough for you?" Carlo asked. "Sensor scan indicates she's fully loaded, too."

Yana whistled, then grinned. Ships seized under the terms of a letter of marque were considered prizes. Privateers sold their cargoes to the Jovian Union for a small profit, with the Earth corporation that owned the prize paying a ransom for the return of ship and crew.

"Whose starship?" Yana asked. She didn't mean the freighter out there in the darkness. In the specialized language of starship crews, she was asking who was currently in charge of the *Comet*.

"My starship," Tycho said. "Carlo can fly the ship, but I'm keeping the helm."

"You've done what, two intercepts?" Carlo objected. "That's a big prize out there, Tyke. Mom's not going to like it if she gets away."

"Don't call me Tyke," Tycho said. "My watch, my

starship. If you can't follow orders, go back to your cabin."

Yana began buckling the harness that would hold her in place if the *Comet* maneuvered quickly or took damage. Her usual station was starboard of Tycho's and was typically used for monitoring sensors and engineering. She glanced up from untangling her shoulder straps to shake her head at her brothers.

"Quit fighting, boys," Yana said. "Mom's gonna take over anyway. Want me to run sensors, Tycho?"

"Please," Tycho said, grateful that his sister didn't also feel like challenging his authority.

"I've got sensors, Vesuvia," Yana told the *Comet*'s computer. She peered at her scope. "Distance to target eight thousand klicks."

The ladderwell rang with new footsteps as their parents, Diocletia Hashoone and Mavry Malone, descended to the quarterdeck from the crew quarters above. Diocletia gathered her black hair into a hasty ponytail as she looked over Tycho's shoulder.

"It's an Orion—fully loaded, no transponder code yet," Tycho told his mother. "Seven and a half thousand klicks."

"Why do prizes always have to come during the middle watch?" asked Mavry with a yawn and a stretch, sitting down at the first mate's station on the starboard side, forward of Yana and across from Carlo.

Diocletia said nothing, her eyes leaping from the main screen to the other scopes. Three minutes ago she'd been sound asleep; now her brain was swiftly taking in sensor and navigation data, drawing conclusions, and making plans.

"Do you want the helm, Captain?" Tycho forced himself to ask, trying not to make it obvious how badly he wanted her to say no.

His mother said nothing. She took five steps forward and sat in the captain's chair, behind the console closest to the bow. She snapped her fingers, and her instruments came to life.

"Captain on deck," Vesuvia announced, and Tycho waited to be relieved of command. But his mother surprised him.

"Your starship, Tycho," Diocletia said. "Let's see if you've been paying attention."

2

TYCHO AT THE HELM

Diocletia turned back to the main screen, leaving responsibility for the *Shadow Comet* in Tycho's hands. He swallowed nervously. The quarterdeck was cool, yet he could feel himself beginning to sweat.

"Seven thousand klicks," Yana said. "You okay over there, Tyke?"

Carlo glanced back over his shoulder. Tycho glared at his sister.

"I'm fine," he said. "You just keep reading off distance to target."

Diocletia Hashoone had been captain of the *Shadow Comet* for eleven years, having taken over from her father, Huff Hashoone. One day, in turn, she would name one of her children to succeed her. So while Tycho, Carlo, and Yana were crewmates and had to work together, they were competitors, too—the *Comet* could have only one captain. And that meant all three were constantly being tested.

When Carlo or Yana was in command of the *Comet*, Tycho of course wanted them to succeed: every prize taken was more money for their family and helped the Jovian Union in its struggle against Earth. But he didn't want them to do *too* well and hurt his own chances at the captain's chair. Ideally, something would go wrong—something that wasn't bad enough to endanger the ship and their lives, but bad enough that their mother would notice and remember. But that was a dangerous game. In space, things that went wrong had a way of proving fatal.

Tycho shook the thought away. Now it was his turn at the helm, and Carlo and Yana's turn to hope he did well but still made a mistake or two.

"Engine status?" Tycho asked.

"Green across the board," Carlo said, indicating that all systems were working normally.

"Detach tanks and take us out, Carlo—intercept course," Tycho said. "Vesuvia, get me Mr. Grigsby."

Carlo flipped switches on his console with practiced ease. Above them, the Hashoones heard a metallic clank, then felt a bump as the *Comet* separated from the bulky fuel tanks she used for interplanetary voyages. The tanks dwarfed the ship, which was a slightly elongated triangle about sixty meters long, widening from her narrow bow to the three maneuvering engines protruding from her stern.

Beneath his feet, Tycho felt the thrum of the *Comet*'s thrusters rise in pitch as Carlo accelerated out from behind the jumble of rocks and dust that had hidden the ship.

"Grigsby here," a harsh voice crackled over his speakers.

"Mr. Grigsby, this is the helm," Tycho said. "Remind the gunnery crews they are not to fire unless fired upon."

"Aye, Master Hashoone," Grigsby said, recognizing Tycho's voice. "She's a prize, then, Captain?"

"Not sure yet," Tycho said. "If she's Jovian, we'd better not put a hole in her. And if she *is* a prize, let's take her intact."

Tycho hesitated, imagining the *Comet*'s warrant officer standing at his communications unit in the wardroom belowdecks. "Better the condition, bigger the shares. Isn't that right, Mr. Grigsby?"

Out of the corner of his eye, Tycho saw his father smile.

"Right you are, Master Hashoone," Grigsby said. "We'll be ready."

Carlo fed extra power to the *Comet*'s starboard engine and accelerated, banking the ship to port. Ahead, through the viewports, the approaching freighter grew into a brighter dot against the glittering stars.

"Five thousand klicks," Yana said.

"Hail the freighter on all channels," Tycho said.

"Channels open," Mavry said. "Go ahead, Captain."

Tycho hesitated. "You don't want to hail her, Dad? Mom?"

Diocletia turned in her chair, eyes narrowed.

"Your starship," she said.

Carlo shook his head, amused, and Tycho felt his face flush. He nodded and fitted his headset over his ears, then checked to make sure that he was transmitting.

"Freighter, identify yourself," Tycho said.

The communicator crackled with static.

"Four thousand klicks," Yana said.

"We're lawful traders with a schedule to keep, unidentified ship," a gruff voice finally responded. "Why don't you identify *yourself*?"

Tycho shut off the external microphone.

"Vesuvia, display colors," he said.

"Acknowledged," the ship's artificial intelligence said, activating the *Comet*'s transponders so they broadcast her true identity and allegiance.

"This is the *Shadow Comet*, operating under letter of marque of the Jovian Union," Tycho said, reactivating his microphone and trying to make his voice as deep as possible. "I repeat, identify yourself."

"Why didn't you say so in the first place?" the freighter's captain asked. "We're Jovian too—this is the *Cephalax II* out of Ganymede."

"Transponders report Jovian Union allegiance," Yana reported, one eyebrow arched skeptically.

"It's a trick," Carlo said.

Tycho checked that his microphone was shut off. "Of course it's a trick," he said, annoyed. "Just keep us warmed up for intercept."

"Three thousand," Yana said.

Tycho turned his microphone back on.

"Nice to see you out here, *Ceph-Two*," he said. "Once you transmit the current Jovian recognition code, we'll accept your pass and see you on your way."

There was a long pause. The Hashoones looked at one another.

"Our communications antenna suffered some damage on the voyage to Earth, *Comet*," the captain said. "I'm afraid our codes aren't up-to-date."

"Sorry to hear that, *Ceph-Two*," Tycho said. "We'll also accept last month's code."

"Two thousand klicks," Yana said.

"*Comet*, our antenna problems short-circuited our transponders," the captain said. "Afraid we can't transmit."

"Wow, at least come up with a good story!" said Yana.

"Belay that," Diocletia ordered, giving her daughter a sharp look.

Tycho had heard enough.

"*Cephalax II*, we claim your vessel under the articles of war governing interplanetary commerce," he said. "Shut down your engines and prepare for boarding."

"You sound barely old enough to shave," the captain scoffed. "You want me to surrender my freighter to a kid?"

"A thousand klicks," Yana said.

Tycho keyed his microphone again.

"No, *Ceph-Two*, I want you to surrender to the pair of twenty-gigajoule laser cannons this kid has locked on your vessel," Tycho said, trying to make his voice sound cold and ruthless. "Heave to or we *will* fire."

"Seven hundred fifty klicks," Yana said.

"Mr. Grigsby, you may fire upon my mark," Tycho said.

"Who in the name of space is Grigsby?" the freighter captain demanded. "That your dad?"

Startled, Tycho realized he hadn't switched his microphone to the channel used for communicating with the gunnery crews belowdecks. His last message had gone out into space instead.

"Mr. Grigsby is our warrant officer, *Ceph-Two*," Tycho said, trying to recover his dignity. "He's the man who's going to start putting holes in your hull if you don't shut your engines down *now*."

Tycho switched his microphone to the correct setting. "Mr. Grigsby, you may fire upon my mark—but *only* on my mark."

"Aye-aye, Master Hashoone. Guns are hot," Grigsby growled.

"Five hundred," Yana said. They could see the approaching freighter now, a collection of boxy containers connected by thick steel struts. At her stern sat a quartet of giant spheres—long-range fuel tanks like the ones the *Comet* had temporarily left drifting back among the space rocks.

"Carlo, lock in a starboard intercept course," Tycho said. His heart was thudding. "We'll destroy her sensor masts first. Maybe then she'll take us more seriously."

"Four hundred," Yana said.

"*Ceph-Two*, this is your final warning," Tycho said.

He glanced quickly around the quarterdeck. Carlo had his hands on the yoke, flying with his usual confident ease. Yana was adjusting her instruments, scanning the freighter for any signals that might hint at hidden weapons. Diocletia and Mavry stared straight ahead, watching the freighter close the gap between them. All were ready—for battle, boarding, or whatever might come next.

"Hold your fire, *Comet*," the freighter's captain said disgustedly. "We're powering down."

"Good choice, *Ceph-Two*. Shut down all flight systems and prepare to be boarded." Tycho shut off his microphone. "Yana, what are they doing?"

"Velocity dropping," Yana said. "Ion emissions at trace levels. They're shutting down."

"Mr. Grigsby," Tycho said, again double-checking that he was hitting the right switch. "Keep your eyes open, but easy on the guns. Prepare the boarding party."

"With pleasure, Master Hashoone."

Clomping sounds came from the ladderwell, like the impact of hammers on the hull. But this sound was familiar to Tycho. He turned in time to see his grandfather, Huff Hashoone, skip the last three rungs and crash to the deck. As retired captain of the ship, Huff had no station of his own. That didn't bother him—he liked to stand between Yana's and Tycho's stations, his metal feet magnetized to hold him in place during difficult maneuvers.

Nearly half of Huff's body was metallic parts—reconnecting everything had made him the last to arrive. His right forearm was gleaming chrome, ending in a wicked-looking blaster cannon screwed into his artificial wrist, while his lower legs were dull black metal. His gray hair hung long over a face that was half scarred flesh and half a chrome skull in which an artificial eye blazed white. The skin he had left was covered with tattoos—mermaids and skulls, as well as names and symbols whose meaning none of the Hashoones knew. Huff no longer ate—a power cable plugged into a metal socket in his throat. Above the socket, a green light indicated his cybernetic systems were fully charged.

"A prize! I can almost smell it!" Huff roared. He patted three carbines tucked into a cracked black harness that stretched across his chest, letting his organic hand linger lovingly on the wicked-looking pistols, then gripped the pommel of his sword.

Diocletia looked at her father and cocked an eyebrow.

"Are we invading Earth, Dad?" she asked.

"A pirate is always prepared!" Huff said. He tromped forward to stare at the main screen, now filled by the port side of the freighter.

"We're not pirates—we're privateers," Diocletia said.

"Word games, Dio," Huff said with a dismissive wave of his blaster cannon.

"Please do not use hand signals that involve swinging a fully charged weapon on the quarterdeck," Vesuvia objected.

"Avast," said Huff. "Belay that, you cursed chatty machine."

"You're staying here," Diocletia told her father. "Tycho has the helm and will lead the boarding party."

"Tyke?" Huff whirled and stared at his grandson in surprise. His artificial eye whirred as it changed focus. "But he's only a lad!"

"We're twelve. How old were you when you led your first boarding party, Grandfather?" Yana asked.

"Arr, I was ten," Huff muttered, pulling at his beard. "But the solar system was different then, girlie."

"Quiet, both of you," Diocletia said, turning to look at Tycho. "Tycho, everything will go fine if you show the crew you're confident," she said. "And if everything doesn't go fine . . . stay behind them and let them do their jobs."

"I will," Tycho said, wishing his voice wasn't quavering.

"Good," Diocletia said. She frowned and turned back to the main screen. "You'd better get going, then. Vesuvia, my starship."

BOARDING PARTY

As he hurried to the lower decks of the *Comet*, Tycho's boots clattered on the rungs of the forward ladder-well. It was a different world down here: the air was thick with smoke and the smell of fuel, and red light dimly illuminated a maze of beams and girders. A few minutes earlier, most of the crewers had been asleep in hammocks strung from those beams. Now they were rushing to their stations, arms cradling weapons and gear.

A female crewer with a shaved, tattooed head and earrings up and down both ears caught sight of him and nearly dropped her wicked-looking laser rifle in her haste to salute.

"Master Hashoone on deck!" she yelled.

The crewers snapped to attention and saluted, their eyes fierce.

"As you were," Tycho said. "Boarding party, assemble at the port airlock."

A cluster of crewers yelled eagerly and rushed in that direction. Hurrying to keep pace with them, Tycho momentarily felt very small—they were big, tough men and women, with scars and artificial parts accumulated over years of fighting. Then he reminded himself that most of them had served his family for their entire lives, and some came from families that had done so for generations. He might be only twelve, but he was a Hashoone—and that meant the family retainers would follow his orders and give their lives for him.

The knot of crewers parted, and Mr. Grigsby stepped forward. The *Comet's* warrant officer was big enough that his head almost touched the security cameras hanging from the ceiling. Grigsby had dark brown skin, white dreadlocks, and tattoos that glowed green, orange, and blue. Strings of gold coins hung from his holsters and jangled as he walked.

"Boarding party of eight, Master Hashoone," he said, then handed over two gleaming chrome laser musketoons. "And here are the ranking officer's weapons."

"Thank you, Mr. Grigsby," Tycho said, taking the heavy guns. They had broad, bell-like muzzles and felt deadly in his hands. He said a silent prayer that he wouldn't have to use them.

Grigsby and the crewers were looking intently at him, he realized. *Stop daydreaming!*

"She's an Orion freighter, fully loaded," Tycho said, his voice breaking on the final word.

Tycho caught a couple of the crewers trying not to smile and raised his voice, staring fiercely at each of the men and women in the circle around him.

"Her captain didn't much like being ordered to shut down," Tycho said. "But that's his tough luck, isn't it? If he doesn't give us trouble, we won't bring him any. But if he starts something, we'll finish it. That clear?"

"Clear," Grigsby said, showing a grin full of chrome teeth.

"Three cheers for Master Tycho!" a crewer yelled, and a moment later all the crewers were cheering, guns and swords raised.

"Dobbs! Richards!" Grigsby bellowed. "Take point!"

Two of the *Comet's* biggest, meanest crewers stepped forward. Both wore plates of armor across their chests. Dobbs, the *Comet's* skinny, ghostly pale master-at-arms, had an evil-smelling cheroot clutched in his teeth. Richards, a belowdecks veteran, stopped at the airlock door, eyes narrowed.

Tycho activated his headset. "Quarterdeck, we're ready."

"You are green for boarding," his mother said coolly in his ears as the bells began to clang, signaling 0300 hours. Tycho waited for the sound of the sixth and final bell to die away, then nodded to Grigsby.

"Open her up," he said.

Alarms sounded and lights flashed as the *Comet's* inner airlock doors began to grind open, followed by the outer airlock doors a few meters away. Beyond them, the hatch of the *Cephalax II* waited. The chill of deep space filled the vestibule, and the vapor of the crewers' breath wreathed their bodies like smoke.

Richards stabbed a finger at the control, using his other hand to hold his carbine at shoulder height, and pointed at the hatch. Tycho held his breath. This was the most dangerous moment of any boarding, when no one knew what waited on the other side of the hatch. If the freighter's crew had decided to resist, the air would soon be filled with laser blasts, smoke, and screams.

"Easy!" Tycho warned, even as he switched off the safeties on his pistols.

The *Cephalax II's* hatch opened with a groan of metal, and wind fluttered through the airlock as the atmospheres of the two ships began to mix. No shots came their way. The freighter's inner airlock doors were already open, and two unhappy-looking men in dirty uniforms waited on the other side, hands held carefully above their heads.

Dobbs and Richards patted the men down for weapons as the *Comet's* other crewers rushed forward, guns at the ready. They glanced quickly down passageways, on guard against an ambush, but for now there was no resistance.

"*Comet*, we're aboard," Tycho said into his headset, then nodded to the *Cephalax II*'s crewers. "Take me to the bridge."

The *Cephalax II* was a pretty typical freighter—neither her passageways nor her crew were particularly clean or neat, but she struck Tycho as being in good working order. The thrum of her power plant was low and steady, and the air smelled stale but clean, indicating her recycling systems were functioning. While the *Comet*'s crewers fanned out through the freighter in pairs, Tycho and Grigsby followed the *Ceph-Two*'s crewers to her bridge. There they found four men sitting at their stations, hands held still and in plain sight, while another man stood beside the captain's chair, staring out the viewport.

"Captain Wofford of the *Cephalax II*, registered on Earth to the GlobalRex Corporation," the man beside the chair said without turning.

Tycho strode across the bridge to the captain's chair. Grateful to know that the imposing Grigsby was right behind him, he took a deep breath and prayed he wouldn't stumble over the lengthy speech the law now required him to deliver.

"Tycho Hashoone, acting as captain of the *Shadow Comet*. According to the laws of war and abiding by Article 23c of the interplanetary accords on space-borne commerce, I claim this craft on behalf of the Jovian Union.

She and her contents will be apportioned according to the laws of space as adjudicated by the Ceres Admiralty Court. By the dictates of our letter of marque, I swear no harm will come to craft or crew."

With this speech complete, he placed his hand upon the captain's chair. Wofford knew what those words and that gesture meant, and Tycho waited for him to accept them and acknowledge that the freighter was now Jovian property.

But instead, Wofford shook his head.

"Afraid you can't do that, kid," he said.

Tycho realized Wofford was looking behind him. He turned and saw one of the freighter's other crewers stand up at his station. He was bearded and thick chested, with hard eyes and a nasty smirk.

"Well, go ahead, Mr. Soughton," Wofford said with a frown. "Present your credentials."

"Right." Soughton lifted a hand to the breast pocket of his uniform shirt. Grigsby raised his carbine, and a dot of red light glowed ominously on Soughton's temple.

"Go slow, matey," Grigsby growled. "Less yer tired of havin' a head."

"Don't get excited," Soughton said. He dug in his pocket and extracted a rumpled document.

"Allow me to present my, uh, credentials as a registered diplomat, acting on behalf of the elected government of Earth," Soughton said, then paused and frowned. "Based on the . . . I mean, according to the laws of war, this craft, her crew, and her contents are protected against seizure by diplomatic immunity."

The corner of Soughton's mouth jerked upward. Grigsby snatched the papers from the man's hand, keeping the red dot fixed on his temple, and handed them to Tycho, who studied them briefly. Soughton crossed his burly arms, smiling.

"You don't look much like a diplomat," Tycho said doubtfully, looking at the muscles bulging under Soughton's greasy uniform.

"And you don't look much like a pirate, kid," Soughton replied with a sneer.

"Privateer," Tycho muttered. He looked helplessly around the bridge, then activated his headset.

"*Comet*, it's Tycho."

"Have you secured the bridge?" his mother asked.

"Yes. Well, sort of. I'm not sure."

"What does that mean?" Diocletia demanded. "Have you secured the bridge or not?"

"We've got a problem," Tycho said.

4
THE MYSTERIOUS DIPLOMAT

Leaving Grigsby to guard the *Ceph-Two*'s bridge, Tycho returned to the *Comet*, Soughton's papers in hand. He spread them out on his mother's console for his parents and siblings to study, while Huff stalked around the quarterdeck, spinning his carbines and arguing with Vesuvia about safety.

"They're fakes," Carlo said. "Anyone could make papers like these."

"No, they're real. Look at this holo-seal," Mavry said

unhappily. "If the authorities on Earth started allowing freighter captains to forge diplomatic credentials, no diplomat of theirs would be safe."

"But Dad, it doesn't make sense," Tycho objected. "What's a diplomat doing on a cruddy freighter instead of a fancy courier ship? Plus he stumbled over the immunity declaration. It was like he'd never said it before."

"So maybe he's new," Yana said with a shrug. "New and inexperienced."

"But he wasn't scared of Grigsby—and *everyone's* scared of Grigsby," Tycho said. "And his uniform was a mess. You've seen Earth diplomats on Ceres, Yana. They walk around in fancy clothes, like they own the solar system."

"Earthfolk, bah," interjected Huff. "Noses pointin' to the sky, every one of 'em. They think they're better 'n us. Don't you believe it, lad."

Huff looked down at his hand and grimaced, then opened and closed his fingers.

"Is your hand hurting, Grandfather?" Yana asked.

"Arr, it's nothin'," Huff said, embarrassed. "Cold on the quarterdeck, is all."

"We could contact the Securitat," Carlo suggested, referring to the Jovian Union's intelligence service.

Diocletia shook her head.

"They'll err on the side of caution and say to let her go," she said. "After all, it's not *their* prize."

Diocletia tapped the holographic seal on Soughton's documents.

27

"I agree that these papers are real," she said. "But like Tycho, I want to know what a diplomat is doing on a beat-up cargo hauler like the *Ceph-Two*."

"Not to mention why he looks more like a Port Town roughneck," Tycho said.

"Does it matter what he looks like?" Mavry asked. "If he's a diplomat, he's a diplomat. We're already risking a fine for interference with interplanetary commerce."

"I know—but this doesn't feel right," Diocletia said, frowning at her husband. "I can't put my finger on exactly what, but something's wrong here."

"I can solve yer problem," Huff said, bringing his built-in cannon down on the console with a clang. "Have yer diplomat take a short walk out the airlock. We'll see what he has to say when he's breathin' vacuum!"

"That's barbaric," objected Carlo, but Huff just grinned a horrible half-living grin, his cybernetic eye a spark of white.

"We will do no such thing," Diocletia said, glaring at her father. "Our letter of marque requires us to abide by the laws of war, as you know perfectly well."

"To say nothing of our responsibility as civilized people," Carlo added.

Huff uttered a foul oath under his breath.

"Dead men don't bite, Dio," he said. "Piracy was glory, before politicians turned it into pushin' papers. Never thought I'd see my own children make a mockery of the family tradition."

"That's enough, Dad," Diocletia said wearily, reaching for her headset.

"Mr. Grigsby, ready the *Ceph-Two* for passage to Ceres," she said. "Carlo will join you as pilot, while First Mate Malone prepares the list of what's in her cargo hold. I want engines lit in twenty-five minutes."

"Aye-aye, ma'am," Grigsby said over the feed. They could hear loud protests behind him, on the bridge of the captured freighter.

"Mr. Grigsby, put Captain Wofford on the communicator before he hurts himself," Diocletia said with a smile.

"What part of diplomatic immunity do you not understand, *Comet*?" the freighter captain demanded.

"The part where old scows carry diplomats who can barely form an official-sounding sentence," Diocletia said. "We're taking your ship to Ceres, where we'll let the admiralty court sort things out."

"This is an act of war, *Comet*," Wofford sputtered. "The fines will wipe out your performance bond even if your ship isn't seized by the authorities."

"We'll see about that, *Ceph-Two*," Diocletia said. "Are you going to be cooperative, or do you need to make the voyage locked in your quarters?"

"I'll go there myself—and I'll see you in court," Wofford said. "The lot of you are no better than common pirates."

"We're far less than that," Huff grumbled. "That's the shame of it."

"We're not pirates, *Ceph-Two*. We're privateers,"

Diocletia said. "Fortunately for you, I might add. *Comet* out."

Diocletia cut the transmission and turned to regard her family.

"Tycho, you *always* check your microphone status before sending a transmission," she said, frowning. "What if the prize had heard you saying something else—warning the crew that we were losing power to the guns, for instance? And how many times do I need to tell you that the first rule of an intercept is to secure the prize's engine room and communications mast? You put the entire intercept at risk by failing to remember that. Now write up the interrogatories for admiralty court, and make sure you include *every* detail of what happened."

Vesuvia's computer memory contained a special section accessible only to the captain. It was known as the Log, and the records in it covered some three hundred years of voyages, under the command of dozens of captains. Everything Tycho, Yana, and Carlo did—good or bad—was entered into the Log. Tycho had a pretty good idea which category the intercept of the *Cephalax II* would fall into. He looked at his feet, defeated.

"Yes, Captain," he managed, then stood there and waited for the silence to end. But it went on, horrible and apparently endless, while Carlo and Yana tried to hide their happiness.

Then he felt his father ruffle his hair.

"But those things aside, you did a good job," Mavry said.

Tycho looked up hopefully.

"Yes, you did—*those things* aside," Diocletia said. "You dealt with the situation on the bridge professionally, and you showed leadership with Grigsby and the crew. Well done, Tycho."

"Thank you, Captain," Tycho said, fighting to keep the smile off his face as he returned to his own station. But he couldn't help it. Yes, he'd made mistakes, but the ship and its cargo were theirs. Yana wrinkled her nose at him, and he felt his happy, relieved grin grow even wider.

Tycho lay in his berth, listening to the thrum of the *Comet*'s engines and staring at the gray metal of the upper hull above his head. When he'd joined the bridge crew, he'd scratched his initials in the paint above his head, adding his own to those left by Hashoones who had called this cabin home before him.

Four bells—it was 0600. Tycho gave up on trying to sleep. He couldn't stop replaying the intercept in his head, fuming at what he'd done wrong and trying to think of any possible explanation for why there'd been a diplomat aboard.

He got up and activated the control for the cabin door, which retracted into the wall. The *Shadow Comet*'s top deck was divided into seven cabins. His parents shared the captain's stateroom in the bow. Aft of that were two unused cabins. One hadn't been touched since his aunt Carina had abandoned it eleven years ago, while the other was used as an office. Then came the cabins belonging to Tycho and to Carlo, with the forward ladderwell leading down to the quarterdeck interrupting the passageway between their doors.

Aft of that, the passageway was split in two by an enclosed ladderwell connecting the top gun turret to belowdecks, with doors to the cuddy and galley on either side. If Tycho kept going aft, he'd find the head, an equipment bay, cabins belonging to Huff and Yana, the aft ladderwell, and a small auxiliary hold reserved for particularly valuable goods.

As Tycho had hoped, his father was in the cuddy, where the bridge crew ate, reviewing documents and drinking coffee from a thermos. Mavry looked up from his mediapad and gave his son a smile, inviting him to sit.

"You should get some sleep," Mavry said. "It's a couple of days to Ceres."

"I tried, Dad," Tycho said. "But I can't."

"I understand," his father said. "After you lead an intercept, it takes a while for your mind to stop going a hundred thousand klicks an hour."

"Yeah, exactly," Tycho said with a grateful nod. He was thankful it was Mavry there in the cuddy and not Diocletia. He loved his mother, but she was the captain and the keeper of the Log—in which, for all he knew, his doubts and fears might be recorded.

"How long was it before your mind stopped doing that afterward?" Tycho asked.

"Stopped doing what?" Mavry asked.

"Running like crazy after intercepts."

Mavry smiled. "Oh, it still does," he said. "Every time."

Tycho looked surprised, then nodded.

"So what's on your mind?" Mavry asked. "Or should I guess? Microphones, engine rooms and communications masts, and what in the name of the Galilean moons a diplomat was doing on that bridge?"

"That's pretty much it," Tycho said.

"And how all this will look in the Log," Mavry added.

Tycho didn't say anything but looked down at his lap, embarrassed.

"Let me put your mind at ease there, at least," Mavry said. "None of us knows what to make of this Mr. Soughton. It's as much a mystery to your mother and me as it is to you. There's no penalty for having to deal with a mystery, Tycho—and you handled it as well as any of us could have. Certainly better than your grandfather would have."

"I guess," Tycho said. "But I can't stop thinking about it anyway. And I know I shouldn't always think of it . . . but how am I doing? You know, overall?"

Mavry took a long swallow of coffee.

"I'm not the captain, Tycho," he said.

"I know, Dad," Tycho said. "But you must have some idea."

"I'll give you my opinion, if you really want it," Mavry said. "I doubt it will be a surprise."

Tycho nodded.

"You're not the best pilot, or the best at reading tricky sensor readings, or a gunnery expert," Mavry said.

"That's pretty much every real job on the *Comet*," Tycho said, trying to keep his voice calm. "I mean, what's left? I key in navigation and run communications. Baby stuff."

"Don't be overdramatic," Mavry said. "Remember that a captain has to be able to handle every job on the ship. You're not great at piloting or sensors or gunnery, but you're not *bad* at these things, either. I'd trust you to handle any of them. For someone who's been a midshipman for only four years and bridge crew for two, that's pretty good."

"Really?" Tycho asked.

"Really," Mavry said.

"But how do I compare to—" Tycho began to ask, only to see his father shaking his head, a stern look on his face.

"I'll always tell you how I think you're doing," Mavry said. "What you're asking now, though, that's the captain's business. You understand that, right?"

"Yeah, I do," Tycho said. "Thanks, Dad."

Mavry nodded.

"You want more advice?" he asked, then leaned forward, as if he were about to tell Tycho a very important secret.

"Get some sleep," he whispered.

5

ADMIRALTY COURT

When the moons of the outer solar system seceded from Earth's government and formed the Jovian Union, the dwarf planet Ceres and several of the more populous asteroids remained independent, refusing to take sides. Nearly a thousand kilometers in diameter, Ceres was the largest inhabited body in the asteroid belt, the vast field of debris located between the orbits of Mars and Jupiter. Centuries before, it had been a jumping-off point for the human race's exploration of the outer planets. Now it remained a hub frequented by traders and explorers, as well as neutral ground for the warships of Earth and the Jovian Union.

For the short trip down to the surface of Ceres, the Hashoones boarded the *Shadow Comet*'s gig. Tycho peered out the porthole as Carlo undocked the gig from the *Comet*. Everywhere he looked, he saw starships—needle-nosed scout ships, great slab-sided galleons, bat-winged warships, bulbous tankers, and even a gaudy passenger liner or two. Smaller ships buzzed around them—packets, tenders, avisos, and gigs like theirs, all taking crewers to and from the mottled orange-and-white globe below.

"Pirate's dream, ain't it, lad?" growled Huff in his ear. Tycho jumped and saw that his grandfather had leaned forward from the seat behind him to look out the porthole, no doubt calculating the wealth aboard all those ships out there.

Tycho nodded and pulled nervously at his tight collar. The Hashoones had traded their usual shipboard jumpsuits for tunics and button-down shirts, the dress code for admiralty court. Huff had dug up an old tie in a slightly terrifying shade of yellow. He had removed his forearm cannon, leaving a metal stump with an empty socket in it. The socket twitched and spun, trying to follow Huff's thoughts and find something to shoot at.

"Yana, don't scuff up your shoes," Diocletia said from her seat in the front of the gig beside Carlo. She hadn't turned around to deliver this warning—she had heard the little thuds and scrapes of her daughter kicking at the deck two rows behind her and identified what they were. Yana caught Tycho glancing her way and bugged her eyes out slightly. Each knew what the other one was thinking: How did their mother sense these things? Was that part of being a captain? If so, would they ever learn to do it?

"While we're dirtside, pay attention—not just in admiralty court, but in the rest of the port as well," Diocletia said, still looking forward to scout the ships surrounding them. "Don't think you're off duty because you're not aboard the *Comet*. A lot of cruises succeed or fail because of something that happens in port, not space."

The surface of Ceres was a maze of tunnels and pressure domes filled with merchant warehouses, provisioning yards, hydroponic greenhouses, repair shops, kips, eateries, and grog houses, advertising their wares with everything from 3D holographic displays to ancient neon tubes. Everywhere you looked there were people: gawking tourists, hurrying merchant spacers, watchful naval officers in Earth or Jovian uniforms, grimy miners, sharp-dressed officials, and hard-eyed men and women who looked like their professions might not be entirely legal.

The Hashoones shouldered their way through the crowds between their landing field and a pair of broad doors made out of actual wood, with brass fittings. Uniformed guards stood to each side. This was the Ceres

Admiralty Court, where disputes about the laws of space were heard and decided upon.

Tycho had been to admiralty court before, and it always disappointed him that the inside was so little like the outside. After passing through those grand wooden doors, you found rows of metal benches and two plain tables reserved for the principal figures in each side of a dispute, facing the judge's raised podium and a screen of fake potted plants.

Diocletia sat down behind one of the two tables at the front of the room and indicated that Tycho should sit beside her. Mavry patted his son's shoulder as he took his own seat in the row behind them, next to Carlo and Yana. Huff scanned the room suspiciously before sitting beside Yana, a difficult operation that involved whining motors and clattering metal parts.

At the other table sat Soughton, crammed into an ill-fitting suit that was shiny at the elbows. Beside him sat a slim bald man in a much fancier-looking suit made of iridescent material. Captain Wofford and other members of the *Cephalax II*'s crew sat on the benches behind them, along with a bunch of men and women Tycho had never seen. He figured they were Earth bureaucrats who worked for GlobalRex, the massive corporation that owned the *Ceph-Two* and, it seemed, a good chunk of everything else on Earth.

A door opened behind the judge's podium, and the Honorable Uribel Quence entered, followed by a uniformed bailiff. Quence was sweating profusely, as usual.

Everyone in the courtroom rose and remained standing until the judge settled himself in his chair, grabbed his white wig before it could slide off in a slick of perspiration, and banged on his desk with a gavel. The Hashoones were familiar with the admiralty court judges: Quence was brisk and fair, and had little patience for fools.

Unfortunately, Tycho had no idea what "fair" would mean today. None of the Hashoones did.

"We've done nothing wrong, so just answer whatever questions the judge asks you," Diocletia whispered. "But follow my lead—if I start talking, be quiet and wait."

Tycho nodded. Judge Quence looked at the mediapad on his desk and frowned, the expression dragging wattles of loose flesh down below his jaw. Then he looked up, and his eyes fell on Tycho.

"Master Hashoone," he said. "I didn't expect to find you in my courtroom quite so soon. You're a precocious lad. So this is your prize, then?"

"Yes, Your Honor," Tycho managed, aware of how many eyes were upon him.

"And have you brought me a copy of your letter of marque, interrogatories from the intercept, and your condemnation order?" Judge Quence asked.

"I have, Your Honor," Tycho said, getting to his feet and hearing his chair scrape across the floor. He brought the sheaf of papers to the judge's desk and stood there, staring awkwardly at Quence's powdered wig while he waited.

"The bailiff will take those, Master Hashoone," Judge Quence said after a moment, without looking up.

Tycho heard people laugh behind him. He turned and saw the bailiff waiting with his hand extended, face impassive. Tycho gave the man the papers and scurried back to his chair.

"Thank you, Master Hashoone," Judge Quence said. "You may now transmit electronic versions for the record."

Diocletia turned to Mavry, who nodded and punched commands into his mediapad. Judge Quence stared down at his own device for a time, then looked up and pursed his lips.

"Master Hashoone, am I reading this correctly?" he asked. "You intercepted a freighter in the outer asteroid belt, discovered she was carrying an accredited Earth diplomat, and brought her to Ceres as a prize anyway?"

Before Tycho could speak, the bald man in the expensive suit was on his feet, turning first one way and then the other to survey the courtroom.

"That's exactly right, Your Honor. This is a most distressing case." The man's voice was bright and friendly, carrying easily from one end of the courtroom to the other. "As you'll find from our own documents entered into the record, the *Shadow Comet* has violated the terms of her letter of marque by ignoring a clear case of diplomatic immunity, a deliberate and extraordinary event that must be swiftly and severely punished. On behalf of Captain Hans Wofford, the GlobalRex Corporation, and His Majesty's Sovereign Government of Earth, I ask Your Honor to impose penalties against her performance bond for piracy and interference with commerce, and to recommend charges against her crew of kidnapping and multiple counts of illegal operation of a starship."

Judge Quence peered out at the man, who was standing confidently before the table with his hands behind his back.

"Are you Master Hashoone?" Judge Quence asked.

"No, Your Honor," the man said. "Allow me to—"

"If you're not Master Hashoone, then why are you speaking?" Judge Quence asked.

Huff brayed laughter.

"That there is the biggest stuffed shirt this side o' Neptune," he growled to Carlo, loud enough for Tycho to hear. Judge Quence gaveled him into silence as Diocletia spun and gave her father a poisonous look.

"Now, Master Hashoone, what's the meaning of all this?" Judge Quence asked.

"Well, Your Honor—" Tycho began, but then his mother laid her hand on his.

"If I may, Your Honor?" Diocletia asked.

Judge Quence nodded, and Diocletia pointed over at Soughton, who sat smiling behind the other table.

"That man does indeed have diplomatic credentials," she said. "But we don't believe he's a diplomat."

"Your Honor, if I may—" exclaimed the man in the fancy suit, springing back to his feet.

BAM! went the gavel. Judge Quence's wig slid a couple of inches to the right.

"You may *not*, sir," Judge Quence said. "Captain Hashoone, if a man has diplomatic credentials, does that not make him a diplomat? I'm aware the question borders on the philosophical, but . . . you do have credentials, correct, Mr. Soughton?"

Soughton got to his feet, a folder in his hand, and walked slowly to the front of the courtroom, where Quence indicated he should hand the folder to the bailiff. Judge Quence then reached for it, flipped it open, and began to read.

"What's going on?" Tycho asked his mother in a whisper, but she put her finger to her lips.

"Your Honor," the man in the fancy suit tried again.

"You seem determined to speak, sir," Judge Quence said. "Very well. Who are you, exactly, and what are you doing in my courtroom?"

"My name, Your Honor, is Threece Suud," he said in that smooth voice. "Allow me to present my own credentials, which you will find as proper as those of my colleague, Mr. Soughton. It is my pleasure to be newly posted to Earth's consulate on Ceres as His Majesty's Secretary for Economic, Diplomatic, and Legal Affairs. I will be representing both Captain Wofford and Mr. Soughton here today."

Tycho looked questioningly at Diocletia, who shrugged.

"He's an Earthman, all right," Huff growled. "Lots of fancy talk when plain speech would do."

Judge Quence gaveled for order once again, sending his wig sliding left and back into its original position.

Tycho peeked back to see Huff muttering and tugging at his yellow tie.

Threece Suud was talking again, marching back and forth at the front of the courtroom, waving his hands with each point he made.

"I have rarely seen such a flagrant violation of the laws of space," he said. "When the illegal interception was made, the *Shadow Comet* was commanded by a twelve-year-old boy—a minor who should have been in school, not behind the guns of a pirate ship."

Tycho felt his face grow hot.

His mother was on her feet, a bright rose of color in each cheek.

"Your Honor, my family has operated the *Shadow Comet* for two hundred and thirty-eight years. On top of everything else, I'm supposed to listen to this man tell me how to run a starship?" she demanded. "Besides, the *Comet* is no pirate ship, as he knows perfectly well. We are privateers operating legally on behalf of the Jovian Union, in accordance with—"

"I withdraw the characterization," Suud said airily. "But changing one word does nothing to change the facts of the case, Your Honor. Which are that—"

BANG! went the gavel.

"Your views are quite clear, Secretary Suud," Judge Quence said. "You should know, however, that in this region of space it's not uncommon to find young boys— and girls, too—serving aboard starships."

"Point taken, Your Honor, however unfortunate the

practice may be," Suud said. "It grieves me to see a child's formative years thrown away as some sort of apprentice criminal."

"Criminal?" demanded Huff, getting to his feet with a roar and ignoring both Diocletia's hisses for him to quiet down and the sharp reports of Judge Quence's gavel. "Tyke here is a far finer boy than any of you pampered, pretty Earthfolks! Why, if I had my laser cannon, I'd show this insolent pup what 'criminal' means!"

"Grandfather, be quiet!" yelped Yana. "You're going to get us into trouble!"

Huff subsided, muttering.

Threece Suud smiled a rather oily smile.

"Your Honor, it seems appropriate to add menacing to the long list of charges pending against the Hashoone family," he said.

"Denied," Judge Quence said. "It was so noisy in here I couldn't hear exactly what was said. But I'll have no further outbursts in this courtroom. Is that understood, Huff?"

Huff muttered something that Judge Quence chose to interpret as a yes.

"Mr. Soughton, stand up, please," the judge said.

Soughton got to his feet, arms folded.

"Your Honor, I will speak on behalf of—" began Suud.

WHAM!

"Secretary Suud, first you speak when I am addressing Master Hashoone, and now you speak when I am talking to Mr. Soughton," Judge Quence said. "Please get control of whatever identity crisis it is that you are having. Now then, Mr. Soughton, how many years have you been with Earth's diplomatic service?"

Suud tugged at the larger man's jacket and whispered something in his ear.

"About three weeks, sir," Soughton said.

"You may address me as Your Honor," Judge Quence said. "Before your three weeks of service, Mr. Soughton, how long was your diplomatic training?"

"Your Honor, let me say that—" Suud said.

BANG!

"What has happened to this courtroom today?" Judge Quence asked in exasperation. "You will speak only when spoken to, Secretary Suud. Mr. Soughton, please answer my question."

"Got no such training, sir," Soughton said. "I mean, Your Honor."

Threece Suud started to get up, then thought better of it and sat back down.

"I see," Judge Quence said. "And what was your occupation, Mr. Soughton, before you joined the diplomatic service?"

Soughton shrugged. "This and that, Your Honor."

"This and that?" Judge Quence asked, incredulous. "What was your most recent place of employment?"

Soughton glanced at Secretary Suud, who nodded.

"Working for Carnegie-Frick Ventures, Your Honor," Soughton said.

Tycho had never heard of that. He looked at his mother, but her face was impassive.

"Thank you, Mr. Soughton," Judge Quence said. He looked down at the papers on his desk, then peered out at the courtroom and saw that Suud had his hand in the air.

"Yes, Secretary Suud?" Judge Quence asked.

"Your Honor, Mr. Soughton's length of service with the diplomatic corps is not at issue here," Suud said. "Nor is the nature of his prior employment. His credentials show him to be a legally accredited diplomat of Earth, and those credentials entitle him and any starship transporting him to diplomatic immunity."

"I understand that, Secretary," Judge Quence said. "What I don't understand is why people who have done 'this and that' are suddenly becoming diplomats. Is a diplomatic career so little valued on Earth that it's being taken up as a hobby? No, don't answer, Secretary Suud. I've heard quite enough for one day."

Judge Quence scanned the papers on his desk again and rubbed his eyes.

"It's all very curious," he said. "I need to think about it. Mr. Soughton, you are released, as is Captain Wofford and the crew of the *Cephalax II*. Captain Wofford, you are ordered to transfer your cargo to an orbital warehouse. It will be held in escrow pending a resolution of this case."

Wofford looked at Judge Quence in horror.

"But Your Honor, that's all my profits for this voyage!"

"I'm aware of that, Hans," Judge Quence said. "Just as you are aware that Earth and the Jovian Union remain technically at war, and privateering is a legal part of that conflict, whatever Secretary Suud's opinion of the matter."

Judge Quence thumbed through his mediapad for a moment, then nodded and looked up.

"Principals in this case are ordered to return three weeks from today," he said, then banged his gavel a final time. "Court dismissed."

6

CERES PURSUIT

W ell, that was interesting," Mavry said with a smile as the Hashoones sat in a cheap café not far from the admiralty court's polished wooden doors. Tycho was reminding himself to sip the carton of sugary jump-pop he'd bought instead of gulping it, while Yana was picking at a plate of dried fruit. Carlo blew on a thimble-sized cup of expensive coffee, while their parents warmed their hands on larger, cheaper cups.

"So we won't find out if she's a prize for three weeks?" Tycho asked worriedly.

"Maybe not even then," Diocletia said. "We're all in uncharted space here."

She rubbed her eyes, frowning, then took a long sip of coffee. Mavry put his hand on her shoulder.

"Anyway, put it out of your mind. There's nothing to be done about it," she said.

"Your mother and I have to file the paperwork with the local Jovian Union offices," Mavry said. "Wait here until Huff gets back, then go with him to the victualing yard and restock the *Comet*'s provisions."

"Where did Grandfather go, anyway?" Yana asked, pulling her mediapad out of her bag.

"He said he was getting a nip of grog," Mavry said from behind his coffee cup.

"How much is a nip?" Carlo asked.

"It varies," Mavry said with a grin, putting down his empty cup and getting to his feet. "Anyway, keep your communicators on—and stay out of trouble."

Tycho watched them vanish into the throng of spacers. Yana was pestering Carlo for a sip of his coffee.

"A *tiny* sip," Carlo warned. "This cost me half my shore allowance."

Yana handed the cup back, her face twisted in dismay.

"Ugh, bitter!" she complained, then returned to scrutinizing her mediapad.

"Don't be such a kid," Carlo said with a laugh. "What are you reading, anyway?"

"The court documents Suud filed," Yana said.

"Anything interesting?" Carlo asked. They all had mediapads, but only Yana's seemed to be permanently attached to her hand.

Yana narrowed her eyes at her brother. "Read them yourself and find out."

"Maybe I will," Carlo said, then glanced at Tycho. "And what are you mooning over?"

Tycho didn't want to say, but now Yana had put her mediapad aside and was looking at him too.

"It's *my* prize. Why did they go to the Union offices without me?" he asked.

"It's not your prize—" Carlo began.

"It was mine in admiralty court!" Tycho snapped.

"Tyke, *relax*," Carlo said. "It was your prize in admiralty court because you were the watch officer and it was your starship during the intercept. It's Mom's prize according to the Jovian Union because she's the captain. Got it?"

Tycho nodded, and after a moment Carlo nodded back.

"Anyway, I don't know why you two keep worrying yourselves to death over the Log," Carlo said. "We all know I'm going to be captain."

"Oh, we do, do we?" Yana asked scornfully. "And how do we know that?"

"Common sense," said Carlo. "I'm the oldest, and I'm the best pilot. I can fly rings around you both—Mom knows it, and we all know the Log shows it. It's nothing to be ashamed of. I'm just saying that the sooner the three of us understand what will happen, the sooner we can start working together more effectively as a bridge crew."

"Aunt Carina's older than Mom, and she's not captain," Tycho pointed out. "She was a better pilot than Mom, too. Or at least that's what everybody says."

"Aunt Carina was going to be the captain, and we all know it," Carlo said. "What happened didn't have anything to do with age or piloting."

"You mean 624 Hektor, don't you?" Yana asked, poking at the last little bits of fruit. "Strange how one day can change everything."

Tycho and Carlo exchanged a surprised glance. The Battle of 624 Hektor was rarely discussed among Jovians. In the minds of many privateers, the mere mention of it invited the worst kind of luck, even eleven years later.

Carlo hesitated, then plunged ahead, as if Yana's mention of the forbidden name had changed the rules.

"It took a lot less than a day—everything changed in a few minutes," Carlo said. "The Martian freighters entered the asteroids, our pirate ships moved to intercept them from where they'd been waiting in ambush, and then the Earth ships that had been hiding in the asteroids powered up and ambushed *us* instead. By the time the Jovian Defense Force showed up, most of our ships had been destroyed or crippled."

"Because we were betrayed," Yana said.

Carlo shrugged. "That's the story."

"You sound like you don't believe it," Tycho said.

"Depends on which part you mean," Carlo said. "Do I believe some of our fellow Jupiter pirates sold us out? Yes, I do. Do I believe the Jovian Union let us get massacred so they could gain control of the survivors? No way—it's a crazy conspiracy theory."

Neither their parents nor Huff had ever talked about the terrible moment when missiles fired by an Earth destroyer had ripped through the *Comet*'s quarterdeck. Diocletia, Mavry, and Carina had escaped serious harm, but Huff had nearly been killed, suffering injuries too great for him to continue as captain. The thought still chilled Tycho during solitary watches. He imagined the blare of warning sirens, the impacts like hammer blows, and then the scream of air escaping through holes in the hull, dragging along with it anything not secured into space.

"At least Grandfather survived," Carlo said quietly after a moment. "A lot of pirates didn't. Stearns Cody. Helga von Stegl. Thane D'Artagn."

"And Sims Gibraltar," Yana muttered. "Aunt Carina's fiancé."

Carlo nodded.

"What ship did Sims serve on again?" Tycho asked.

"The *Ghostlight*," Carlo said. "A direct hit cracked her reactor, spilling radiation everywhere. His family took him back to Ganymede, to care for him as best they could. When Aunt Carina heard he'd died, she swore she'd never go into space again. And so the captain's chair went to Mom."

The Hashoones had repaired the *Comet*—you could still see the pale spots where the quarterdeck's hull had been patched with new steel. But things had changed by the time she returned to deep space. In the aftermath of 624 Hektor, the Jovian Union formally outlawed piracy— but then swiftly offered letters of marque to some of the surviving pirate captains. Diocletia had aspired to be the captain of a pirate ship, but the *Comet* had become a privateer, a lawful commerce raider.

A table of freighter bums behind them laughed uproariously, clanking tumblers of something vile-smelling. Yana lifted her head from staring at her plate.

"Well, I don't need a disaster to become captain," she said. "I'll beat you out fair and square, Carlo."

Carlo smiled and shook his head.

"And me?" Tycho asked.

"Oh, like I need help beating *you*," Yana said.

Before Tycho could reply, Carlo shushed them.

"Quiet—Grandfather's here," he said. The Log and the *Comet*'s captaincy were sensitive subjects with their grandfather, but no subject was more sensitive than 624 Hektor and its aftermath.

Huff didn't come over to their table. Instead, he stood just inside the door to the café and bellowed at them, causing heads to turn at every table.

"Hurry up, you lot—we're late!" he thundered. "Can't wait around fer yeh all day, y'know!"

"And whose fault is that?" Yana asked Tycho with a grin as they got up from the table.

He glared at her, still angry.

"Oh, come on, Tyke," Yana said, rolling her eyes. "I was joking. Don't be so *serious*."

They got their bearings in the crowded passageway outside the café. Huff looked mournfully down at the stump of his mechanical wrist.

"Wish I had me persuader," he grumbled. "Ceres ain't wild like it used to be, but seems there's always some young punk what wants to cause a ruckus."

"Nobody's going to mess with you, Grandfather," Yana said, and Huff brightened.

"Come on," Carlo said. "Let's get to the yard and see about getting the *Comet* resupplied. Before Threece Suud decides that's illegal, too."

They shouldered their way through the throngs of spacers, ignoring the come-ons of the shop fronts' holographic displays.

"What do you think Judge Quence will decide?" Tycho asked his grandfather.

"Don't know much about lawyerin' and don't care to learn," Huff said, fixing a band of passing roughnecks with a glower. "But ol' Quencie, he's a sensible sort, been around the solar system a time or two. Pirate once upon a time, even."

"Judge Quence was a pirate?" Yana asked in disbelief.

"Oh, sure. First mate aboard the *Dead Hand*, 'fore she crashed on Thelxinoe," Huff said. "Quencie mostly stayed on the right side of the law, stuck to runnin' freight, but he'd fly with a black transponder when it suited him.

Got in a scrap with him once or twice myself, when I was captain."

"Why'd he quit?" Tycho asked.

"You'd have to ask him, laddie," Huff said. "One day we heard he'd shipped off to Mars to get himself a fancy law degree. Yeh want my opinion, though, it's that Uribel never much cared for being shot at—took it *personal*."

"Ex-pirates shouldn't be judges," sniffed Carlo.

"And why's that?" asked Huff. "If a body's going to sit in judgment of others, better he's lived a little, not wasted his life in a courtroom."

"Because we need laws, Grandfather," Carlo said. "And if you've broken them before, you're in no position to enforce them later."

"Arrr, belay that," said Huff. "Laws don't come floatin' out of deep space, boy. They're made by folks. Some of them's good folks, some not so much, and laws are like children—they look like the folks what made 'em. Remember the reason we Jovians is fightin' Earth, Carlo. I know you've heard lots of high-falutin' talk 'bout why, but comes down to some unfair folks made some unfair laws way back when, and ever since then Earth folks been too stubborn to admit they're wrong and undo 'em."

"But Grandfather—" Carlo said.

"But nothin', Carlo," Huff said. "You seen that Mr. Suud—sounds like he wants to outlaw privateerin', or make it impossible. A generation ago the solar system was full of pirates, and now there's just a handful of us left. Suppose they took privateerin' away too. What would you do? Dock the *Comet* an' leave her to rust?"

"You're being overly dramatic, Grandfather," Carlo said. "It wouldn't come to that."

"I bet everybody thinks that, before things change," Yana piped up.

Huff nodded at Yana, his mechanical eye bright in his face.

"Arrr, that they do," Huff said. "That they do."

They were waiting in line outside a chandler's depot when Yana gave a start of surprise.

"Look!" she said.

Tycho looked, but saw nothing unusual—just the normal crowd of spacers.

"That man over there—he was at admiralty court, sitting behind Suud," she said. "Suud spoke to him after court was adjourned. It looked like he was giving him orders."

"Which man?" Huff asked.

"The one with the mustache," Yana said.

"I don't recognize him," Carlo said doubtfully.

"That's because you weren't paying attention," Yana said. "Remember what Mom said about the importance of things that happen in port? I gave everybody on that side of the room a good once-over. It's him—and he wasn't on the *Ceph-Two*."

"So he's Suud's aide," Carlo said. "So what?"

"Look at the guys he's with," Yana said. "Do they

look like Earth bureaucrats to you?"

Tycho didn't recognize the man, who was wearing the sort of drab tunic you saw many places on Ceres, as was the man next to him. Tycho couldn't say for sure *what* he looked like. But Yana had a point about the others. Everything about them—from their rolling gait to their numerous earrings, tattoos, scars, and missing parts—suggested they didn't work at desks but made their living in space. They might be freighter bums with colorful pasts, but they might also be pirates, or even slavers.

"Obviously they're diplomats," Tycho said, which won him a bark of laughter from Huff.

"If that Soughton's a diplomat, I'm the eighth sultana of Mars," Huff said. "Looks like an old-time leg breaker, that one does. Back when pirates ruled space, the old Earth shipping firms used to send their haulers out with toughs aboard—thugs what were half pirate themselves. They'd keep the cargo from vanishing and watch for any crewer that might have a mind to be contactin' pirates."

"Pirates like you, Grandfather?" Yana asked.

"Aye," Huff said with a grin. "We intercepted plenty of prizes on account of some underpaid crewer sharing a route in port for a little cash. And why not? Weren't his cargo, and the shipper would pay the ransom to get ship and crew back, with nobody getting hurt. 'Twas a more civilized way of doing business."

The men, still deep in conversation, continued along the vaulted corridor toward the next pressure dome.

"We have to follow them," Yana said.

"What we have to do is get provisions for the *Comet*," Carlo said.

"This is important," Yana said. "I know it is! Hurry— they're getting away!"

"We don't all need to stand in line, Carlo," Tycho said. "Yana and I will follow them."

Carlo shrugged. "Suit yourselves," he said with a smile. "While you play amateur detective, I'll be following my captain's orders."

"Fine with me," Yana said.

"Not so fast, lassie," Huff said. "I'm goin' too."

"No, Grandfather," Yana said. "They'll notice you— and besides, your indicators are flashing yellow."

"Arrr, so they are," Huff muttered. "I got too worked up back in the courtroom. Be careful, you two. Anything happens to yeh, yer mother'll have the half of my head what's still flesh and bone."

"We will be," Yana promised. "Come on, Tyke!"

"Keep your communicators on," Carlo called after them as they hurried down the tube.

Yana spotted Suud's aide and his companions, and she and Tycho angled their way through the spacers and workers to get closer. They followed them through one of Ceres's larger pressure domes, passing the gilded wooden facade of the Bank of Ceres, and then down another tunnel, this one built under the dwarf planet's surface of loose rock and ice.

"Where do you think they're going?" Yana asked Tycho.

"Beats me," Tycho said. The lower levels of Ceres were mostly living quarters—kips and hostels, along with shops and bars.

"I'm telling you, there's something funny going on here," Yana said. "And I bet it has something to do with our court case."

"You might be right," Tycho said. "But don't get too close. If the crowd thins out, they'll spot us right away."

"Good point," Yana said. "I wish we weren't wearing our court clothes. They stand out in a crowd *and* I hate them."

Suddenly both their communicators began to chime.

"Oh, no," Yana said as she and Tycho activated their headsets. Their father's voice filled their ears.

"Captain's orders—everybody wrap up what they're doing and return to the landing field," he said. "We're prepping for immediate liftoff."

Carlo's voice came over the feed. "What's going on, Dad? Anything wrong?"

"Nothing's wrong," Mavry said. "In fact, we're invited to a party. A party on Ganymede. We'll tell you more when you get here. *Comet* out."

"Come on, Tyke, we can still follow them a bit longer," Yana said, striding off after their targets.

"No, we can't," Tycho said, hurrying to catch up with his sister. "You heard Dad—immediate liftoff."

"It'll take at least an hour to round up everybody from belowdecks," Yana objected.

"Right, but we're not from belowdecks—we're bridge

crew," Tycho said. "And our captain has given us a recall order."

Yana made a disgusted sound. "Fine," she said. "But first I'm going to get that guy's picture."

She fumbled in her duffel bag without breaking stride, pulled out her mediapad, and raised it in the air.

"Yana, what are you—HEY!" Tycho yelped as his sister shoved him hard sideways, sending him lurching into a heavyset spacer wearing the uniform of a Martian shipping line.

"Watch where you're going, kid!" the man yelled as he and Tycho disentangled themselves.

"Sorry!" Tycho said. The spacer muttered a final warning and stalked off. Yana grinned at her brother as she stashed the mediapad in her bag again.

"Okay, we can go," she said. "I got a perfect shot of the guy we were following when he turned around— and the guys next to him too."

"Are you crazy?" Tycho asked. "That means they saw you!"

"Pfft, they didn't even look at me. They were too busy looking at *you*," Yana said. "And before you freak out, you were blocked by that big beast of a Martian spacer."

"What are you going to tell Mom?" Tycho asked.

"Zero," Yana said. "It might be nothing."

"But what about Grandfather and Carlo?" Tycho asked.

"Grandfather's already forgotten," Yana said. "And unless he thinks it's trouble for us, Carlo doesn't care about anything that doesn't involve Carlo."

"Meanwhile, you could have gotten me killed!" Tycho said.

"Now who's being dramatic?" Yana asked. "Quit looking sore—you got shoved into a Martian, so what."

"It was a bad idea," Tycho muttered as they began the long walk back to the landing field.

Yana just grinned again.

"Silly Tyke," she said. "The only bad ideas are the ones that don't work."

7

DESTINATION JUPITER

A s Yana had predicted, it took more than an hour for the *Comet*'s retainers to make their way back from the various watering holes where they'd been spending shore leave. With the *Comet*'s bosun yet to return, Diocletia assigned Tycho to wait at the airlock, checking names against the roster as shuttles, tugs, and taxis docked with the *Comet* and discharged the roughnecks and brawlers who made up her belowdecks crew.

The Hashoones had warned their retainers that prize money from the *Ceph-Two* might be a while in coming, if it came at all. But from what Tycho could see, few had listened. A number returned proudly showing off new earrings or tattoos, while others carried boxes and parcels—gifts for sweethearts and children waiting for them on the moons of Jupiter. Even those who'd been more careful with their money were weighed down with food, a welcome change from the burgoo and flummery that were shipboard rations. Tycho saw strings of sausages, stacks of sweet cakes, fish snacks for the ship's cat, and everywhere a rainbow of fruit—which spacers loved despite how expensive it was. Grigsby gave him a huge grin around a mouthful of peach, the juice running down his chin and under his collar.

Tycho assigned the latecomers to the blacklist and whatever punishment Grigsby thought appropriate, then clambered up the forward ladderwell to the quarterdeck, where the other Hashoones were waiting at their stations. Diocletia had her hands on her hips, clearly impatient to get going.

"Full complement belowdecks, captain," Tycho said. "One broken arm from a dockside brawl, which the surgeon has already set, but all hands fit for duty."

"Excellent," Diocletia said. For a privateer's entire crew to return from shore leave with only one broken arm was pretty good.

"Are we really going to a party?" Yana asked.

"Yes, we really are," Diocletia said. "The Jovian

Union's defense minister has asked us to return for a meeting at Callisto Station, after which there's a gathering of the Union leadership at Ganymede High Port."

"Arrr," said Huff. "Stuffed-shirt Jovians thinkin' they wanna be Earthfolk. Wish I could space the lot of them."

"It's true, Mom," moaned Yana. "Those things are always so *boring*."

"*Those things* are important to the people who provide us with our letter of marque, which means they're important to us," Diocletia said. "And of course you'll all be on your best behavior. *All* of you."

"Of course we will be," Yana said, offering a pretty smile that she didn't even try to make look convincing.

"All right," Diocletia said. "Well then—two days on Callisto, then on to Ganymede."

"Two days?" asked Carlo sharply. "Why did you give us an immediate recall order if it means we have to spend two days mooning about at home?"

Diocletia turned on him, eyes narrowed.

"Because Ceres and Jupiter are in alignment for only another ninety minutes," she said. "Miss that launch window, and we'll burn five percent more fuel. I'd expect a pilot to know these things."

Carlo lowered his eyes, embarrassed. Yana grinned at Tycho.

"So what's the meeting about?" Tycho asked, trying to change the subject.

Carlo glanced at him, surprised.

"That's between me and the defense minister, Tycho,"

said Diocletia. "Have you calculated our course to Jupiter orbit?"

"Verifying headings," Tycho said. "Should only take another minute."

"Good," Diocletia said. "Take us up to the fueling ring, Carlo."

"Aye-aye, captain," Carlo said. The thrum of the *Comet*'s engines rose in pitch, and the deck beneath the Hashoones' feet began to vibrate. Tycho felt a gentle push back into his seat as the *Comet* rose in a graceful curve from her parking orbit around Ceres.

Ships visiting port left their bulky long-range fuel tanks high in orbit, meaning every planet and important moon in the solar system wore a permanent necklace made up of bulbous tanks, lumbering fuel tankers, and gunboats on patrol. Carlo smoothly guided the *Comet* through traffic, then cut the throttle and eased the ship up into the familiar cradle of struts beneath her own tanks. The Hashoones heard a series of sharp bangs from above.

"Stabilizers engaged," the mechanical voice of Vesuvia said. "Connecting fuel lines."

"Nice flying, Carlo," Mavry said.

Carlo smiled and offered his father a little salute.

"Fuel lines connected," Vesuvia said.

"My board's green," Carlo said.

"Our heading to Jupiter orbit is locked and verified," Tycho said. "Navigational pathways green."

"Sensors look pretty as emeralds," Yana said.

"'Green' will do, Yana," Diocletia said, examining her own systems. "Mavry?"

"Green," Mavry said with exaggerated care, which earned him a sharp look from his wife.

"Vesuvia?" Diocletia said.

"All systems are operational," Vesuvia said.

"Excellent," Diocletia said. "Light her up, Carlo."

"Aye-aye, Captain," Carlo said, reaching for his yoke.

Tycho exhaled sharply as the thrum of the *Comet*'s engines rose to a whine, then a howl. The trip to Jupiter was a routine one, but the sound of the privateer's engines kicking in always made his heart beat more quickly.

He risked a glance around the quarterdeck and saw Yana smile as the rumble of the engines intensified. Huff stood by the ladderwell with teeth bared, his metal feet magnetized to the deck.

Tycho felt his own grin spreading across his face, and when the engines ignited and shoved him back in his chair, he couldn't resist a happy "Woo-hoo!"

"Quiet on deck, Tycho," Diocletia barked without turning around. Embarrassed, Tycho hid his grin behind his hand. But as the *Comet* accelerated into the darkness of space, his father looked back, caught his eye, and winked.

The *Shadow Comet*'s engines allowed her to achieve speeds of 2.77 million kilometers per hour, but that still meant the journey between Ceres and Jupiter took nearly a week. Once the *Comet* reached cruising speed, the howl of her engines diminished to a continuous low rumble, and the Hashoones had little to do but wait. Vesuvia would keep the ship on the proper heading, alerting her crew if they were needed.

Unfortunately, that didn't mean Tycho could spend the trip goofing off in his cabin. There was homework to be done, and Vesuvia didn't like the way he'd been doing it. The *Comet*'s computer had sent Diocletia a long message about Tycho's mistakes on his math homework and his dismal score on a history quiz, along with an analysis of his inefficient study habits while on watch.

Sometimes Tycho wished the *Comet*'s computer needed all of her computational power for running the starship, but Vesuvia could do an amazing number of things at once, from keeping guns charged and conducting sensor sweeps to surprising the younger Hashoones with pop quizzes.

Tycho didn't object to the pop quizzes—they were part of a bridge crewer's apprenticeship, and Yana and Carlo were stuck with them too. But Vesuvia's notes never seemed to include the most important details, like how she'd sprung that history quiz on Tycho while he was investigating a potentially valuable chemical signature on a passing asteroid, or how the middle watch was a lot less boring if you spread your homework out over the entire four hours instead of doing it all at once. If criticisms were going into the Log, they ought to be fair.

Halfway through the trip home, though, Tycho felt he'd made enough progress to satisfy even the tough old computer. He'd scored nine out of ten on a navigation quiz, and Vesuvia had approved his essay tracing the tradition of the black transponder back to the Jolly Roger, the skull-and-crossbones flag used by Earth's ancient seagoing pirates. She'd even given him extra credit for noting that some ancient pirate flags were red, and that the name Jolly Roger might have been derived from *joli rouge*, ancient French for "pretty red."

So Tycho was feeling pretty good, until Diocletia and Mavry summoned their children to the quarterdeck one morning. They arrived to the clang of a single bell announcing 0800 to find their father at his usual station, while their mother stood in front of the main screen, arms behind her back.

"Man your stations," Diocletia ordered.

Tycho looked questioningly at Yana, who shrugged.

Diocletia waited until they were buckled in, then began to pace back and forth.

"A starship crew is a team," she said. "Recently the three of you have been so busy thinking about the Log that you've forgotten about that. If the *Comet* gets turned into space dust because you can't work together, everybody loses. What you do individually goes in the Log—but so does what you do together."

Her eyes held each of theirs in turn.

"Still, like any team, different people are better at different things," Diocletia said.

Carlo turned to smile at his twin siblings.

"Pay attention, Carlo," Diocletia said. "Getting too

specialized leads to trouble. All of you have to be able to do everything on this ship—piloting, sensor scans, navigation, docking, remotely operating the guns, intercepts, boarding actions, maintenance, repairs, preparing a cargo manifest, writing up interrogatories, and more. A captain has to be able to do everything and know within a second or two if someone else is doing it right."

Tycho glanced at his brother and sister. Having been rebuked, Carlo was now sitting straight up at his station, nodding at what their mother was saying. Yana had her arms folded, looking annoyed. Tycho tried his best to sit like Carlo.

"So . . . welcome to a full day of simulations," Diocletia said.

Tycho groaned involuntarily, then covered his mouth—a slip that earned him only a passing glower from his mother.

"You'll each start with things we know you need to work on," Diocletia said. "Tycho, you'll begin by simulating intercepts and then work on your piloting. Vesuvia says you're consistently overshooting your targets."

Tycho nodded, and Diocletia turned to Carlo. "Carlo, you'll be working on intercepts too, and then it's on to a few hours of sensor work. You can't depend on Vesuvia to detect anomalies when performing scans."

Diocletia turned to Yana—but stopped when she saw her daughter's face.

"Is there somewhere you'd rather be, Yana?" she asked.

"Don't pretend like I have a choice, Mom," Yana said, glaring back. "I want it put in the Log that I was tested right after pulling a middle watch."

"What I put in the Log is my business," Diocletia said. "Who told you that privateering is fair?"

Yana held her mother's gaze for a long moment, then dropped her eyes back to her console.

"Nobody," she muttered.

"Good," Diocletia said. "It'll be piloting for you, followed by maintenance and manifests."

Faced with a long, mostly dull day, Yana sighed.

"More privateers die because they skip maintenance or do it badly than die in battles," Diocletia said. "You'd all do well to remember that. Mav?"

Their father got to his feet, hands behind his back.

"After your mother and Vesuvia are done with you, it'll be my turn," Mavry said. "We'll end the day with a flight simulation—a re-creation of the Battle of Deep-space Margolis. It's a tough one—our side got pasted. So if that happens to you, things won't be any worse than they were in real life."

"That's a pleasant thought, Dad," Carlo grumbled.

"A pirate is always cheerful," Mavry said with a grin.

"Privateer," Diocletia said.

"Them too," Mavry said, still grinning. "Okay then, kids. Good luck!"

For simulations, the Hashoones donned goggles and headsets, plunging themselves into virtual worlds of

Vesuvia's making—ones they navigated by using each station's pedals and control yoke. Vesuvia started Tycho off with three intercepts in which nothing went wrong, then surprised him with a freighter crew that chose to scuttle the ship rather than surrender to the *Comet's* boarding party, followed by another routine intercept and then an ambush on the bridge.

Next came piloting, which had never felt natural to Tycho. He envied Carlo's confident touch at the controls—for his brother, the yoke was like an extension of his own hands, while Tycho could never stop remembering that the *Comet* was a gigantic machine he was trying to push through space with a tiny lever. He found himself sweating even before Vesuvia started simulating sluggish rudders, engines stuck on full ignition, and other potentially fatal malfunctions.

They ate a quick lunch at their consoles and then got back to work, with a single short break at the midpoint of the afternoon watch. Tycho was exhausted by the time their screens went black and Mavry told them it was time for the Deepspace Margolis simulation. The only bright spot, he thought, was that Yana and Carlo looked tired and unhappy too. He wondered if what Vesuvia had engineered to torment his brother and sister had been as hard as what he'd had to deal with.

"So who was smart enough to look up the Battle of Deepspace Margolis during the break?" Mavry asked.

Yana's hand shot up, and Mavry nodded at his daughter.

"It was in 2649, after the Second Trans-Jovian War," she said. "A task force of fifteen Earth ships ambushed a mixed force of seven Jovian destroyers, allied pirate ships, and freighters."

"That's right," Mavry said. "And who were the commanders?"

Tycho's hand was up. "Admiral Byson for Earth, while Captains Trantolier and Livesey were the ranking Jovian commanders."

"Correct," Mavry said. "And who was at the helm of the *Kuiper Centurion*?"

Carlo didn't even raise his hand. "Martin Luther Hashoone," he said. "Our seventh-great-grandfather."

Diocletia descended the ladderwell and nodded at Mavry.

"That's right," she said. "And what happened to him?"

"He died," Yana said as seven bells sounded.

"Correct," Diocletia said. "The stern of the *Comet* includes three armor plates salvaged from the *Centurion*. Everything else was vaporized. Martin Luther didn't fare too well at Deepspace Margolis. Let's see how you do."

The three young Hashoones put their goggles and headsets back on. Tycho gripped his control yoke as Vesuvia began loading data for each of their simulations. First he saw a starfield and a scattering of asteroids. Then Vesuvia populated the simulation with Earth warships—but there were only nine, not fifteen, and two of them were heavily damaged and listing to starboard. Tycho

"Did you check your history?" Mavry asked. "There were no reinforcements at 153 Hilda—Trantolier and Livesey were forced to commit every spaceworthy ship they had."

"I know that," Tycho said. "But I also know that the *Centurion* was the fourth ship destroyed at Deepspace Margolis, not the last. So I was hoping you'd changed something else in the scenario."

Diocletia nodded. "Very good, Tycho. The strategy didn't work, but it was good thinking."

Mavry turned his attention to Carlo.

"You lasted for four and a half minutes," he said. "Strategy?"

"There was a gap between the center of the Earth formation and the right flank, covered only by one damaged destroyer," Carlo said. "I angled the keel to put as much armor as I could between me and them and tried to shoot the gap."

"And what happened?" Diocletia asked.

"The Earth commander sniffed it out and was able to plug the hole before I could get through," Carlo said. "But I almost made it."

"Almost," Mavry said.

"Almost isn't bad in an unfair test," Carlo said.

Diocletia's eyebrows leaped upward.

"And why was it an unfair test?" she asked.

"There was no way to win," Carlo said.

"And that can't happen in real life?" Diocletia asked,

holding her son's gaze until he looked away. Then she turned to Yana.

"Yana, you lasted—"

"Ninety-eight seconds," Yana said, arms folded.

"And your strategy?" Diocletia asked.

"Aimed all guns forward and headed full throttle into the center of Byson's line," Yana said.

"Where you were destroyed," Diocletia said.

"I destroyed two enemy warships," Yana said. "Neither Tycho nor Carlo had even one kill."

"You destroyed two enemies, yes—but at the cost of your life and your ship," Diocletia said.

Yana shrugged. "Sometimes you're gonna die."

8

DARKLANDS

Tycho didn't figure out what was bothering him until two days after the *Comet* returned to Callisto: his old room didn't feel like his anymore, just like the Hashoone complex no longer felt like home. It was just a place—familiar, but not special beyond that.

Tycho was lying in his old bed, having given up on homework for the moment. The ceiling showed a view from a camera outside—a black sky littered with stars. Callisto didn't rotate—one side of the moon always pointed at Jupiter, while the other faced away from the planet. The Hashoones and all the other Callistan settlers lived on the dark side, using the moon as a shield against the radiation generated by Jupiter's magnetosphere.

Tycho reached over to his nightstand and flipped a control, changing the ceiling to the bright blue sky of a sunny day on Earth. He'd never seen Earth's skies, but the light and the colors comforted him anyway. Humans had evolved in those conditions, and a few hundred years of living under very different skies weren't enough to change what felt natural.

But today, the blue sky just made him more aware of the illusion, reminding him that he was looking at an image projected on a stone ceiling, above which were twenty meters of rock and dirt and then the hostile, frozen surface of the moon.

Tycho decided that looking at the ceiling was a waste of time, so he heaved himself off the bed and left his room, leaning against the railing to stare down into the well of the Hashoones' home. Known as Darklands, it had been built around a mine shaft drilled more than four centuries ago, when the family first came to Callisto as settlers from Earth. The mine had once been rich, yielding enough minerals and pockets of frozen gases to make the Hashoones wealthy, so they could afford a homestead of their own instead of living in the crowded squalor of a settlement like Port Town.

Tycho walked down the ramp that corkscrewed around the outer wall of the old mineshaft, connecting old equipment lockers and storerooms that had been converted long ago to bedrooms and offices. Slabs of rock sealed off the old tunnels. Tycho let his hand trail along the rough rock wall, listening to the echo of his footsteps. He tried to imagine what it had been like in Gregorius Hashoone's day, when the shaft had been filled with the hammering of robotic drills and the shouts of miners in armored suits.

Now it was silent except for the low hum of air scrubbers and the burbling of water pumps. The mine had been exhausted within a century of the Hashoones' arrival, and soon after that, Gregorius's great-grandson Lodovico Hashoone had taken a desperate gamble. He'd armed the family's old ore boats with converted laser drills and promised the family's miners wealth and adventure if they'd bring their carbines and knives and sign on as space pirates. Somehow, Lodovico's plan had worked. The Hashoones' mining days were over.

On the lower level, couches, a table and chairs, and a simple kitchen shared space with a giant steel water tank and filtration equipment. Beneath the tank, Tycho knew, meter-wide pipes descended for nearly two hundred kilometers, tapping into a salty ocean of water and ammonia far below Callisto's crust. Tycho had never liked thinking of that pitch-black ocean somewhere beneath his feet.

Tycho heard a polite cough. He looked up and saw Parsons, who kept Darklands in working condition, standing nearby.

"Do you require anything, Master Hashoone?" the gray-haired man asked, polite and dignified as always.

"No, thank you," Tycho said. "Are Mom and Dad and Aunt Carina back yet?"

"They are still at their meeting at Callisto Station," Parsons said.

Tycho sighed. "It's taking forever. Where's everybody else?"

"Your sister is in the simulation room, working on a piloting exercise," Parsons said. "Master Carlo took the grav-sled on an errand to Port Town. And I believe your grandfather is sitting in the crypt."

"Thank you, Parsons," Tycho said. The man bowed slightly and glided away as Tycho sank onto the couch and drummed his fingers on the metal surface of an end table. He wished he'd known Carlo was going to Port Town. It was a dull huddle of pressure domes and converted mines, not nearly as exciting as Ceres, but it was something.

Tycho looked around, frowning. If he were honest with himself, he had to admit that the complex had never felt like home. He and Yana had spent the first eight years of their lives here, but they'd always known they belonged in space—that learning their lessons and working hard enough to satisfy their aunt Carina was the way to become midshipmen aboard the *Comet*, as Carlo had done. Childhood at Darklands was about waiting until it was your turn to leave.

The quiet unnerved Tycho all of a sudden. The familiar living room somehow felt lonely. Carina had kept only an occasional eye on Carlo, Yana, and Tycho, leaving their raising to a series of governesses, along with invalid pirates too badly injured to return to space. The governesses had long since gone back to Ganymede, the pirates had retired to Port Town, and now there were no Hashoone children left to get in trouble for jumping on the furniture.

Tycho decided not to bother his sister. She'd just be annoyed with him, and the last thing he wanted to think about right now was flight simulations. That left his grandfather, down in the crypt. Tycho had rarely been down there; as a child, he had been frightened by the gloomy chamber.

He hesitated, then carefully descended the stairs to the crypt, softly illuminated by a bluish light. He caught sight of a green square and a white dot in the gloom.

"Hullo, Tyke," Huff said, the white light of his artificial eye turning toward his grandson.

"Would you rather be alone, Grandfather?" Tycho asked.

"No harm in company," Huff said. "Just payin' respects to the departed. Do it whenever we return."

Tycho came and stood next to Huff, who was looking up at a shimmering hologram of a bald man with a sharp nose and a slightly mocking grin.

"That's my father—yer great-grandfather—Johannes Hashoone," Huff said. "Taught me everythin' I know about the pirate trade. Arrr, what a man he was."

"Is he buried here?" Tycho asked.

"Father?" Huff looked surprised, maybe even a bit offended. "No . . . jettisoned into space, as was his wish. We're not for buryin', Tyke. Awful thought for a pirate, spendin' eternity under dirt. When you hear me death rattle, lad, just shove whatever's left of me out into space."

Huff reached for the panel that controlled the hologram, then stopped, grimacing and flexing his hand.

"Tyke, do your ol' granddad a favor and get one of those pills out of my bandolier," he asked.

Tycho did as he was asked, and Huff placed the pill under his tongue gratefully, still flexing his hand.

"Arthritis," Huff explained. "Don't get old, Tyke."

"I hear it's better than the alternative, Grandfather," Tycho said.

Huff rumbled with laughter. "Aye, that it is." He stabbed at the buttons and Johannes's image disappeared, replaced by that of a regal-looking man in old-fashioned clothes.

"That there is old Martin Luther Hashoone," Huff said. "I gather you made his acquaintance, back on the *Comet*."

Tycho winced. "You know about the test, then."

"Aye," Huff said. "Was watchin' on my viewscreen, even."

"So whose strategy did you think was best?" Tycho asked.

"Yer sister's," Huff said at once. "Betcha knew that already. She's got all the instincts to be a fine pirate one day."

"*Privateer*, Grandfather," Tycho said. "And what about me and Carlo?"

"Your plan weren't bad, lad," Huff said. "When you're dealt a bad hand, sometimes it's best to lay back and play for a better card. As for Carlo . . . arr. That one needs to learn that flyin' ain't everything. And captain's summat yeh earn, not summat what gets handed to yeh. A pirate never makes assumptions, Tyke—they'll be the death of yeh."

"I know," Tycho said. He hesitated, then plunged ahead, into dangerous territory: "Anything can happen. Like it did with Mom and Aunt Carina."

Huff was silent for a long moment, and Tycho wondered if he'd gone too far.

"You know I don't talk about that, lad," Huff said at last, staring up at the flickering image of Martin Luther Hashoone. But then he continued anyway—perhaps the presence of his ancestors made more-recent history less painful to confront. "We lost good pirates on that dark day, Tyke. Some of our bravest and boldest. And the reputation of some worthy pirates wound up just as dead."

"The ones who betrayed us," Tycho said.

"Arrr, the very ones," Huff said. "Thoadbone Mox. And Oshima Yakata."

"What happened to them?" Tycho asked.

"Thoadbone ran and hid somewhere around Saturn, tryin' to stay a step ahead of the Securitat's agents—stay ahead of them and any Jupiter pirate he happened to run across," Huff said. "Heard he met his maker a few years back—shot full of holes over Mars. And good riddance."

"And the other one? Osh . . . Oshima?"

"Sold her ship and retired to Io," Huff said. "Ain't seen her since. Don't care to, neither."

They stood in silence for a moment, beneath the gaze of Martin Luther Hashoone.

"Grandfather, do you believe what they say—that the Jovian Union betrayed us too?" Tycho asked hesitantly.

Huff looked at his grandson, then turned to contemplate the shimmering image of their ancestor—a man whose last sight, Tycho realized, might have been the bow of an onrushing warship from Earth.

"Y'know about the jammers, then," Huff said, still staring up at Martin Luther's ghostly form.

"I've heard stories," Tycho said.

"Oh? And what 'ave yeh heard?"

Tycho swallowed.

"That . . . that the Martian convoy was carrying experimental jammers, and the Securitat gave all of you software programs to protect against them," he said. "Except when our ships activated the program, all their systems went haywire and shut down. They were left defenseless."

"Aye, that's it, more or less, lad," Huff said. "The Securitat said agents from Earth had infiltrated their code works and set a trap for us all."

"Do *you* believe that?" Tycho asked.

Huff looked away into the darkness of the crypt,

shoulders slumped. For a moment he seemed shrunken and old.

"'Tis an evil thing to believe, lad. The universe is a hard enough place without doubtin' yer own country-men," Huff muttered into the gloom. "But then, these are hard times."

He straightened up again and turned back to Tycho.

"Them pirates what met their maker that day, they'd tell yeh dead's dead, an' it don't much matter how they got that way," Huff said. "What matters, laddie, is what us folks left behind do with our time. That and what we believe in—family, an' our way of life."

Tycho nodded.

"Remember the old pirate saying, Tyke—the family is the captain," Huff said. "And the captain is the ship."

"And the ship is the family," Tycho said.

"That's right, lad," Huff said, wiping at his living eye with the back of his flesh-and-blood hand. "That's right."

He sighed and reached over to the console, fiddling with it until Johannes Hashoone reappeared.

"What brings yeh down here anyways?" Huff asked. "Yer a mite young for talkin' to ghosts."

Tycho started to object that he was old enough to appreciate their shared family history, then stopped, sensing that his grandfather was really talking about himself.

"I don't know," he said. "I was up in my room, and it didn't feel like my room anymore."

Huff glanced over at him, his artificial eye a pinprick of bright light.

"I miss my cabin, back on the ship," Tycho said. "That's my room, and the *Comet*'s my home—not this place, not anymore. Does that make sense?"

Huff grinned and clapped Tycho on the back, hard enough to knock the breath out of his lungs.

"It sure does, lad!" he said. "Means yer gettin' fuel in your blood! We ain't for sleepin' soft and eatin' dainty, not us! And there ain't no horizon big enough to compete with deep space, Tyke—least not in the eyes of a pirate."

Tycho started to remind Huff they were privateers, not pirates. But instead he shut his mouth and smiled back.

9

HIGH SOCIETY

Diocletia, Mavry, and Carina returned from Callisto Station but said there was no time to discuss their mysterious meeting with the Jovian defense minister. If they were going to be on time for the party at Ganymede High Port, everyone had to get dressed *now*—and "dressed" meant well groomed and not wearing anything wrinkled or scuffed.

Tycho managed to get his tie reasonably straight and smooth out the worst of the wrinkles in his dress tunic, but his mother ignored all that, focusing instead on the seventy-five angles his hair was going in. Fortunately, he wasn't the only one who'd incurred her wrath. She dispatched Parsons to salvage Mavry's rumpled tunic, then whirled to ask Huff how he couldn't have noticed that his mechanical arm's lubricant reservoir was leaking. And then there was Yana, who was refusing to wear her dress. After a couple of rounds fought to a draw, Diocletia left that battle to her sister, while Tycho stood against the wall, happy to be ignored.

It was obvious that Diocletia and Carina were sisters—they had the same dark hair, long, thin limbs, and quickness with a sharp glance—but Tycho thought they looked less alike every time he saw them together. Diocletia's hair was long, her skin was tan from exposure to the unfiltered solar glare of deep space, and her eyes tended to jump around, constantly monitoring her surroundings. Carina, on the other hand, wore her black hair short, and her skin was pale from her subterranean life at Darklands, where she kept track of the Hashoones' finances from her overstuffed office. She had a habit of staring into the distance, teeth worrying at her fingers while her mind seemed to sort through some problem.

With Tycho's hair tamed, Mavry's tunic ironed, Huff's arm repaired, and Yana's rebellion put down, Diocletia assembled the family for a careful once-over while Carlo prepared the ship's gig for the brief flight to Ganymede.

"Can't you at least tell us about the meeting?" Tycho asked once they were aboard, Callisto shrinking to a speckled sphere below them. Outside the viewport loomed the gigantic bulk of Jupiter, striped in white and orange.

"No, because I want your minds focused on the party," Diocletia said. "Your father and I will have our own business to attend to. Tycho, I want you to stick with Carlo. He'll explain who's who and introduce you. Listen and learn."

"Wait a minute," Carlo objected, turning in such agitation that the gig's prow momentarily pitched upward. "Why am I stuck with some kid—"

"I'm not a kid—" Tycho began, but Diocletia cut him off.

"Your brother—who is, after all, a fellow member of the bridge crew—will accompany you, Carlo, because that is your captain's order," she said. "In the meantime, please fly this vessel like it isn't your first time behind a control yoke."

"Liftoff isn't the best time to startle the pilot, Mother," Carlo muttered.

"Far more startling things happen to pilots during liftoff," Diocletia said. "Now, listen—"

"What about me?" Yana wanted to know. "Why am I always left out?"

Diocletia turned, one eyebrow raised.

"You could barely be persuaded to dress properly, and now you're mad that I don't trust you to make small talk with the most important people in the Jovian Union?" she asked.

Yana turned red and picked at the hem of her dress.

"Listen, Yana—and you too, Tyke," Diocletia said. "You're now old enough to go to events that are this important, but you have to know how to behave. Some of the people who are going to be there will think what we do is a great adventure. Those are the easy ones. Answer their questions—without giving away any of our secrets, of course. Emphasize that what we do is legal and that we do it on behalf of the Jovian Union. And be charming."

"And what about the ones who think differently?" Carlo asked. "What about the ones who look down on us?"

"With those, be *more* charming," Mavry said.

Carlo snorted. Yana rolled her eyes, sighed, and resumed her inspection of her dress. Tycho peered out the window, wishing they were going somewhere else. Huff opened and closed his hand, grumbling about stuffed shirts.

"Remember, it's the support of these people that allows us to do what we do," Mavry said. "Without our letter of marque, we're just another pack of freighter bums looking for a break."

High Port was a cluster of habitation modules orbiting Ganymede. The space station's largest dome had been converted to a luxurious reception hall for the Jovian Union's notable visitors. One side of the hall was dominated by massive radiation-shielded windows that looked out over the cratered surface of the moon below and beyond it to Jupiter. The gas giant had rotated so that the huge storm known as the Great Red Spot was visible. It stared out at them like a baleful eye, churning through Jupiter's upper atmosphere as it had for more than a thousand years.

Every bigwig in the Jovian Union seemed to be there. The men wore high-collared tunics, white to suit the formal occasion, while the women wore tunics or dresses of black, red, orange, or yellow. At the center of the gathering stood the Union's president, politely smiling as she received a steady stream of well-wishers. Other clumps of people surrounded key government officials; barons, counts, and earls from Io, Ganymede, and Callisto; and the heads of families made wealthy through mining or shipping. Scattered throughout the room were crisply uniformed officers of the Jovian Defense Force; cold-eyed agents of the Securitat; bearded, uncomfortable-looking delegates from the moons of Saturn and Uranus; a gaggle of rangers from the Protectorate of Europa; and a few men and women Tycho recognized as fellow privateers. And everywhere there were aides, valets, junior officers, waiters, and servants.

Tycho's instinct was to retreat to a distant window and hide, but Carlo saw the panic on his face and shook his head.

"Oh, no, you don't," Carlo said, grabbing his elbow and steering him into the crowd.

"I thought you didn't want to be stuck with some kid," Tycho said angrily.

"I don't, but Mom gave me an order," Carlo said. "Listen and follow my lead. These are important people, so you better not mess up and make me look bad."

He grabbed two juices from a waiter's tray, and they waded into the throng.

"It would be a breach of protocol to introduce you to President Goddard, but I've met Count Tiamat, so we can talk to him," Carlo said.

"Who?" asked Tycho, puzzled.

"Tiamat Sulcus—that's his title, not his name," Carlo said quietly. "It's a region on Ganymede. I'll introduce you before Grandfather shows up to embarrass us."

"Don't talk about him that way!" Tycho said, raising his voice.

Carlo looked around, alarmed, and shushed him.

"Don't be such a *kid*, Tyke," he said. "I love Grand-father—you know that. But the way he acts makes people think we're some kind of criminals."

Tycho started to object, but Carlo had his hand on his shoulder and was guiding him across the room.

"Keep your drink in your left hand—that way you don't shake with a cold hand," Carlo said. "Now look over there. That's Count Tiamat standing with Lord Rafsanjani, the head of Callisto Minerals. They're probably having a really boring conversation about ore purification. You know Lord Rafsanjani—our great-uncle Ulric, the one from the Water Authority, married his daughter Anja after he quit pirating. Next to Rafsanjani is Hugh ap Wyvern, the Jovian resources minister, and his wife, whose name escapes me at the moment. And next to her . . ."

Tycho managed not to say anything too foolish and mostly limited himself to nodding and smiling at the right times, sneaking glances around the party when some important person wasn't speaking to him. His mother and father never seemed to be in the same place twice, moving smoothly from person to person. Huff, he saw, had parked himself near a drinks table, where he was deep in animated conversation with two other old privateers, whom Carlo identified as Min Theo and Lars Harken.

"You're doing fine," Carlo told him as they disengaged politely from a brief chat with a Prospectors' Alliance representative and the son of a Ganymede shipping magnate.

"Now look, there are some people from the Helmsmen's Guild I'd like to talk to by myself—pilot talk, you wouldn't be interested. Would you go find Yana before she gets herself in trouble?"

Tycho wanted to object that he found pilot talk interesting, but Carlo had put up with his assignment with relative good humor, except for that remark about their grandfather. He nodded and let his brother go, then looked around for somewhere he might escape to.

To his surprise, he spotted Yana and Huff talking with Count Tiamat and his wife, a huge woman with tiny fingers hidden by a rainbow of rings. Beside them stood a craggy-faced man in a Jovian Defense Force uniform. Tiamat retainers and JDF aides were hovering

"I wasn't referring to you, my dear," Count Tiamat said smoothly. "I meant those you are forced to associate with in such a business. In the JDF there's the threat of renewed conflict with Earth, of course, but—"

"My goodness, darling, don't be so dramatic," Countess Tiamat said with a theatrical wave that sent bracelets spinning up her arm. Her voice was so loud that Tycho wondered if she was going deaf and was too proud to get an implant. "That's ancient history—it would never again come to such a dreadful pass."

She leaned close to Tycho, a conspiratorial effect quickly ruined by the fact that she was as loud as ever.

"I have many old friends in the Earth diplomatic corps," Countess Tiamat said. "Just the other day, one of them told me Earth has registered *hundreds* of new diplomats. That's a hopeful sign, don't you think? If there must be conflict, let's at least pursue it through diplomacy and politics, not weapons."

"Hmph," said Count Tiamat, his displeasure at being interrupted obvious.

"But let's not talk about such things," Countess Tiamat boomed, then turned to smile at Yana. "Gallivanting around the solar system on some pirate ship is very romantic for you boys, but it's not at all proper for this young lady. My dear, you have no idea what a lovely young woman you're becoming. Why, within a couple of years you'll be the prettiest girl in the entire Jupiter system!"

"I don't want to be the prettiest girl in the entire

Jupiter system," Yana sputtered.

"Then what do you want, my dear?" Countess Tiamat asked, a polite smile plastered to her face.

For a moment Yana looked too speechless with rage to answer. Then she offered Countess Tiamat a little curtsy, cocked her fingers at the ceiling, and smiled.

"I want to be the girl with the most *firepower*," she said.

Countess Tiamat looked like she was struggling to find words. A smile spread across Huff's face, then turned into an explosion of hoarse laughter. Yana blew imaginary smoke from her fingertips, then excused herself and marched off across the room.

"Pardon us, Count and Countess Tiamat, Captain Holloway," Tycho said, and led his grandfather after Yana. Huff was still snorting with laughter. But a moment later they both heard Countess Tiamat's too-loud voice behind them.

"Well what would you expect?" she sputtered. "They can call themselves privateers, but we all know they're just pirates with papers."

Huff came to a sudden halt, the motors in his mechanical legs squealing in protest. He started to turn, the living half of his face bright red, but Tycho grabbed his arm.

"Grandfather, *don't*," he warned.

Huff glowered at him, but then his face softened.

"Yer right, Tyke, yer right," Huff muttered. "Let's find another glass of that fancy Ganymedan Reserve."

With a glass of whiskey and another of fruit juice

secured, Tycho led his grandfather to the window, where he figured any outburst would do the least damage. Huff stared out at the massive globe of Jupiter, still fuming.

"Pirates with papers, arrrr," Huff scoffed. "As if it's our fault we're stuck with papers. What I wouldn't do to keelhaul that old bat. Yeh know how the count of the Galileo Regio met Countess Tiamat's mother, Tyke? She was a cocktail waitress on a luxury liner, that's how. As for Count Tiamat, his grandfather was a prospector who owed money to every merchant in Port Town. And for the record, Tyke, the gun crews on the *Copernican Pilgrimage* couldn't hit the surface of a moon if they fell out of orbit."

Tycho laughed, but Huff was still angry.

"Count Tiamat's kin run the resources ministry, which decides what the Union pays companies for raw materials," he said. "Last year they reduced the price to hurt the count's competitors. Meant lots of miners at those companies lost their jobs."

Huff tossed back the rest of his whiskey and scowled, flexing his hand.

"That's the thing of it, lad," Huff said. "Nowadays some folks think it's honorable to steal with words and computers, but they look down on us for doin' it with cannons. They think they're clean 'cause they don't know the people paid to do their dirty work."

10

THE CYBELE ASTEROIDS

When the Hashoones returned to Darklands, Carina told them to prepare for a family meeting. Fifteen minutes later everyone had found a place around the dining area's big table. It was actual wood from Earth, an heirloom some pirate ancestor had claimed in a long-forgotten exploit. Tycho loved to trace the lines and rings visible beneath the lacquered surface, marveling at the thought that he was touching something that had once been alive.

Most of the Hashoones had happily shucked off some fraction of the night's fancy clothes. Mavry was wearing a ratty T-shirt over his formal trousers, while Yana and Tycho had immediately shed every trace of their formal wear in favor of the loose-fitting jumpsuits they normally wore aboard the *Comet*. Only Carlo and Diocletia still looked ready to rub elbows with the elite—not counting Parsons, serving drinks with his usual quiet elegance.

"You've waited long enough to hear about our meeting with the Jovian Defense Ministry," Diocletia said. "The basics are that the *Shadow Comet* has been given a mission—and after some discussion, we've accepted it. Sixteen Jovian merchant ships have disappeared in the Cybele asteroids over the last few months, and the JDF wants us to investigate."

"The JDF has ships of its own," Carlo said. "Why don't *they* investigate?"

"Because tensions are increasing again with Earth, and they're worried about sending forces that far from Jupiter," Carina said. "And not many of the JDF captains know that part of the asteroid belt as well as we do."

The Cybele asteroids were located on the outer perimeter of the belt, Tycho remembered, short of Jupiter's orbit. Most of the Cybeles were poor in minerals, water ice, and other valuable commodities, making them a little-explored part of the solar system with a reputation for lawlessness.

"Are the ransoms on the missing Jovian crews really high?" Tycho asked.

"That's the thing," Carina said. "No ransoms have been asked for. The ships and their crews have simply disappeared."

"If we go out there, we're likely to do the same," Carlo said.

"Look at it as an opportunity," Diocletia said. "Maybe we don't find the JDF's lost ships, but we do find something else. Mineral deposits, say, or water ice."

"Arrr, we ain't no band of scurvy prospectors," muttered Huff.

"Making a living in space is about opportunity, Dad," Carina said. "You taught us that, remember? If you can find something valuable that you can take without someone shooting at you, that's a good thing."

Huff grunted and dismissed her words with a wave.

"Aunt Carina?" Tycho asked. "Aren't there supposed to be slave camps out there?"

"How many times have I told you not to listen to tall tales while you're belowdecks?" Carlo scoffed.

"Tall tales?" demanded Huff. "What about 171 Ophelia? Or the Tumbles? Them tall tales turned out to be true, lad."

"That was forty years ago, Grandfather," Carlo said. "Sure, there are corporate factories in the asteroids. We all know that, and I wouldn't want to live in one. But the people who work there do so by choice. Slave camps are totally different—and they were all shut down long ago."

"Maybe they were and maybe they weren't, boy. It's a big solar system," Huff said. "But even if there ain't slave camps anymore, folks on Earth and Mars spend their lives working for the same corporations that ran things back then—GlobalRex, Amalgamated Social Graph, the United Collective, the whole lot. Which ain't much better than slavery. And if some on Earth get their way, that'll be our lives too."

Carina held up her hand for calm.

"We don't know what you'll find," she said. "Personally, Carlo, I also doubt there are slave camps anymore—that would bring Earth and the Union perilously close to shooting at each other again. But Father's right—it's a big solar system. You might find factory owners who aren't picky about where their workers come from, or pirates who'd rather dump their captives on some rock than arrange ransoms—I keep hearing about an uptick in pirate activity around Saturn and beyond. Or maybe it's a coincidence, and you won't find anything."

"This is all interesting, but what's in it for us?" Yana asked. "We're not a rescue ship."

"I asked the same question, though a little more politely," Carina said. "The ministry is promising us a stipend while we search, a share of anything we recover—"

"They'll give us a share of anything *we* recover?" Yana asked. "How generous!"

"—and a quick resolution to any problems that might come up with the renewal of our letter of marque," Carina finished, smiling slightly.

All the Hashoones went silent. The only sounds were the hum of water pipes and air pumps and the quiet footsteps of Parsons at work in the kitchen.

"It's blackmail, in other words," Carlo said.

"Blackmail is such an *ugly* word," Mavry said with a grin. "Let's just say the defense minister made a trip into the Cybeles seem like an excellent use of our time."

Carlo started to say something else, but Diocletia held up her hand.

"That's enough. Whatever the circumstances, we serve the Jovian Union and we've agreed to help," Diocletia said. "I've told Grigsby to assemble the crew in Port Town by 0900 hours tomorrow. I want articles signed by all hands by 1100 and engines lit by 1200. Busy day tomorrow—get some sleep."

It was strange, thought Tycho. Unless you were very close to a planet, moon, or asteroid, the solar system mostly looked the same—empty space as far as you could see. This far out, the sun was simply a more intense point of light than the other stars, the planets little bright dots slowly following their courses against the backdrop of the galaxy.

And yet the outer reaches of the Cybeles felt different, Tycho thought. He knew it was crazy, but this area of space felt desolate and abandoned, as if the scattered chunks of rock somehow knew they were slowly tumbling through a portion of the solar system nobody cared about.

Or at least this area of space was *supposed* to be deserted. Somewhere out here they might find secret work camps run by slavers. Or pirates' nests. Or the hulks of abandoned freighters left adrift by their captors for retrieval months or years later.

But they hadn't found any of those things yet—not in a week of slow searching among the asteroids, sensors probing for a hint of engine emissions, a fragment of communications, or an unexpected heat source. As far as the crew of the *Shadow Comet* could tell, they were alone.

They were all tired of it, but Huff had really had enough.

He'd been outraged by Countess Tiamat's insult even before finding out they'd been blackmailed into a rescue mission. He'd taken to standing by the ladderwell with his arms folded, muttering about the foolishness of this trip, when he wasn't arguing with Vesuvia about unsafe operation of his forearm cannon. The rest of the Hashoones felt relieved whenever Huff's power indicators turned red and he had to recharge his cybernetic body in his own cabin.

At the moment, though, Huff's indicators were green and he was mad.

"Arr, ain't nothin' out here but space dust," he growled. "This ain't even lookin' for a needle in a haystack, because there ain't no haystack."

"Belay that talk," Diocletia said wearily. "Yana, target that clump of rocks at thirty degrees. Make sure you scan it for chemical signatures, too."

"Thirty degrees, aye-aye," Yana mumbled, hands

moving automatically over her instruments. "Vesuvia, run a diagnostic check on the chemical sniffers."

"All instruments are functioning normally," said Vesuvia, the only member of the crew who didn't sound exhausted, annoyed, or both.

The engines throbbed momentarily as Carlo tapped the throttle, sending the *Comet* closer to the asteroids with a little puff of exhaust. Somewhere above them, their long-range fuel tanks were drifting slowly through space. Searching each section of the asteroids without them saved fuel and made the *Comet* more maneuverable.

"No chemical signatures detected," Vesuvia said.

"Ion emissions?" asked Yana with a sigh.

"Negative."

"Communications bands?" Yana said.

"Nothing detected," Vesuvia said.

Yana groaned.

"I take it back," snarled Huff. "Ain't even space dust out here. Right now a few grams of dust would seem like the Lost Treasure of the *Maria Abelia*."

The bells tolled three times—it was 1730, nearing the end of the first dog watch.

"Carlo, take us to the next target in this sector—the one at two hundred sixty-five degrees," Diocletia said, conspicuously ignoring her father. "There are some bigger asteroids in that one, plus that anomalous chemical signature we detected yesterday."

"On rescan, that anomaly registered as a miscalibrated sensor," Vesuvia reminded her.

"Of course it did," said Diocletia, rubbing at her tired eyes. "I forgot. Let's check it out anyway."

Mavry took off his headset and stretched, the bones in his shoulders creaking and popping. He looked back at the three kids and grinned.

"If only our fancy hosts back at Ganymede could witness the romance of privateering," he said, half yawning.

Diocletia shot him an annoyed look, and he stifled his yawn.

"Still, kids, don't get sloppy," Mavry said. "Besides, you never know when good fortune will strike. Remember the *Panaclops*, the prospector that found the Diamond Comet of 2855?"

"Every Jovian spacer knows that story," Carlo grumbled.

"Suddenly you're every Jovian spacer?" Tycho asked, glaring at his brother. "I wouldn't mind hearing it again, Dad."

"You only want to hear it because I don't want to," Carlo said.

"Would you rather sit around and wait for Vesuvia to tell us nothing's happening?" Tycho asked.

"That's enough, you two," Mavry said. "The *Panaclops* was on a thousand-day cruise, one of those brutal tours of duty the old-time prospectors used to pull. Five hundred days out on one parabola, five hundred days back on another. Through Day 495, she'd found nothing. Her crew was near mutiny and demanding the captain scrap the second half of the loop and return to Jupiter straightaway. On Day 496, they found a little whisper of a chemical signature, and a couple of hours later they were on the communicator transmitting the claim for the Diamond Comet."

"Day 496, huh?" asked Carlo, smiling in spite of himself. "All right then, let's see what we find."

"Yer forgettin' summat, though, Mavry, my lad," said Huff.

"What's that?" Mavry asked.

"The *Panaclops*'s next cruise," Huff said. "'Twas another thousand-day tour. She had a new captain and crew—the old swabs had all retired to spend their diamond money. They neared the halfway point of that cruise without finding anything either."

Everybody was listening in spite of themselves, Tycho realized. Even Vesuvia was quiet.

"The new crew knew what had happened last time, so there warn't much argument," Huff said. "On Day 471, her throttle control system failed, and she shot off into deep space with her course and speed locked in. She's halfway through the Oort cloud now, with empty fuel tanks and a crew of mummies."

"That's horrible," Yana murmured.

"That it is, missy," Huff said. "Point is, yeh never know which kind of cruise yer gonna get."

Tycho woke with a start. He was supposed to be on watch, but he'd forgotten. Carlo had gone to bed without waiting to be relieved, and Vesuvia must have malfunctioned. He hurled himself out of his berth and ran from his cabin to the forward ladderwell, descending to the quarterdeck in shorts and a stained old T-shirt.

It was too late, he saw at once: the *Shadow Comet* was surrounded by pirate ships. They were so close he could see down the muzzles of their blaster cannons. Before he could yell or move, they opened fire. The temperature of the quarterdeck shot upward, became unbearably hot, and he opened his mouth to scream—

—and woke up, for real this time.

A dream, Tycho thought. *You were dreaming.* He twisted around in his berth to look at the clock affixed to the bulkhead in his cabin. It was just after 0300, the depths of the middle watch.

Except he was awake, and the alarms really were screaming.

"Bridge crew to quarterdeck," Vesuvia said over the *Comet*'s internal speakers. "All hands to stations. Repeating. Bridge crew to quarterdeck. All hands to stations."

The other Hashoones were already on the quarterdeck, except for Huff, who needed a few extra minutes to attach his prosthetic limbs and make sure his systems were operating properly. But to Tycho's relief, his mother and Carlo were still blinking away sleep and Mavry hadn't sat down yet. Tycho was late, but by less than a minute.

"What's going on?" Tycho asked, waiting irritably for his monitor to power up.

"Ion emissions," Yana said. "Still faint, but levels are growing."

"What heading?" Carlo asked, studying his own monitors.

"Coming from deeper in the asteroid belt," Yana said. "Coming hard, if readings are accurate."

"Whose starship?" Tycho asked.

"Mine," Yana said instantly. "Carlo, you're pilot. Tycho, communications. Vesuvia, I need a sensor profile of the incoming craft."

"Data still insufficient to assemble a profile," Vesuvia said.

"Nothing to do but wait, then," Mavry said.

Tense moments ticked by. Yana studied her monitor and frowned.

"Definitely ion emissions," she said. "Whatever she is, she's coming in awfully hot."

The main screen lit up, displaying the positions of the *Comet* and the mysterious ship.

"Calculating," Vesuvia said. "Long-range sensors indicate length of seventy to eighty meters."

"No freighter that small would be all the way out here," Tycho said. "And she's too big to be a prospector."

"My starship," Diocletia said. "Carlo, there are asteroids to starboard. Take us behind them."

"Mom!" Yana objected.

"Not now, Yana," Diocletia said. "Carlo, behind the asteroids. Take it slow, but do it now. Yana, step up your sensor scans. Tycho, monitor transmissions on all wavelengths. I need eyes and ears open."

Carlo pushed the control yoke to the right, and the

Comet curved gracefully through space.

"Mr. Grigsby, we've got a bogey, moving fast," Diocletia said into her microphone. "All guns charged, please, but easy on the triggers."

"Aye, captain," Grigsby replied. "The boys'll be gentle."

They heard the bosun's pipe whistling out the order below, followed by a crash that announced Huff had arrived on the quarterback from above. His artificial eye gleamed white as he studied the main screen, his mind quickly calculating velocity and position.

"Preliminary sensor profile complete," Vesuvia said. "Profile fits Leopard-class frigate, but confidence is limited. Fifty-nine point one percent match."

"That can't be right," Yana said. "Vesuvia, recalculate—"

"Belay that," Diocletia said, peering at her own screen. "She's a heavily modified Leopard, not a standard template. The modifications are throwing the assessment off."

"Arrr, a Leopard," mused Huff. "I wonder—"

"Quiet on deck," Diocletia said. "Vesuvia, is she attached to long-range fuel tanks?"

"Based on extrapolations from current scans, she is not," Vesuvia said. "Confidence level ninety-four point two percent."

"That there's a pirate," growled Huff. "Local one, too. No long-range tanks, burning fuel like a meteor."

"A pirate?" Diocletia asked. "Unlikely."

"I would have picked up her tanks on a scan," Yana said.

"They might still be drifting ahead of us," Huff said. "Or ditched way above or below the ecliptic, out of sight. 'Tis an old trick, Dio—used to do it meself."

"Go to silent running," Diocletia said. "Carlo, kill the engines. Yana, passive sensor scans only. Tycho, double-check that we're flying black transponders. Mavry, shut down the air scrubbers."

For a moment the only sounds were frantic typing and the flipping of switches. Then the lights dimmed on the quarterdeck, and even the rhythmic *shush-shush* of the life-support systems stopped. It was eerily quiet, the main screen glowing a dim red.

"Eight thousand klicks," Yana said. "She's slowing."

Seven bells sounded, the familiar clanging suddenly harsh and startling. The Hashoones leaned forward, peering at their screens.

"She knows we're out here," Huff warned.

"She might at that," Diocletia said. "Tycho, calculate the heading to our long-range tanks and key it in. We might have to leave in a hurry."

"Aye-aye," Tycho said as he typed. "But the calculations will take a few minutes."

"Run away?" demanded Huff. "Avast! Blow her out of space!"

"Let's see what she is before we shoot her full of holes," Diocletia snapped.

As the mysterious ship continued to approach, moving more slowly now, Vesuvia was building a profile of her from what little information the sensors continued to return. The newcomer was slightly larger than the *Comet,* with a needle-nosed bow and arms radiating from thick brackets amidships.

"I know that ship," muttered Huff, scratching his chin with the muzzle of his blaster cannon. That seemed like a terrible idea, and Tycho watched nervously.

Diocletia turned to say something to her father, but before she could, the main screen began flashing red.

"The target has launched several smaller ships," Vesuvia said. "Velocity consistent with pinnaces, fighters, or gigs."

"Yana, distance to target?" Diocletia asked.

"Holding at six thousand klicks," Yana said.

"Arr, I got it," Huff crowed. "She's the *Hydra,* she is."

"Impossible," Diocletia said. "The *Hydra* was destroyed during the Deimos Raid six years ago."

"The target's transponders are active," Vesuvia said. "No image transmitted."

"Ho, a black transponder," Huff murmured, his blaster cannon twitching.

"Incoming transmission," Tycho said. "Audio and video."

"Put it on screen," Diocletia said. "Receiving only—send no transmissions."

Tycho tapped at his keypad and the main screen flickered, revealing a burly man glaring out at them. He was bald, with strings of tears tattooed below the corners of his eyes. His long white mustache had been stiffened with wax until it stuck straight out past his ears. His right ear was studded with alternating diamonds and silver hoops, while his left was a frizzled lump, the center of a web of angry white scars that reached almost to his nose. His left eye was gone, replaced by a black telescoping lens that looked like it had been rammed into his skull.

Tycho had never seen the man before, but his parents' expressions turned grim.

"Thoadbone Mox," Huff said, sounding oddly pleased. "Traitor, slaver, and the lowest, meanest murderin' dog ever to plague the solar system."

"And black sheep of a good Io family, sad to say," Mavry muttered. "Rude of him not to stay dead."

"Unknown ship," Mox said in a voice like gravel and broken glass. "I know you're out there. Show yourself or my hunters will open your hull to space."

Yells of defiance bounced up from belowdecks. Diocletia activated her microphone.

"Mr. Grigsby," she snapped. "Control your crewers!"

The yells were replaced by Grigsby's voice, roaring about scurvy dogs being put in irons. Then all was quiet again.

"Respond or I'll blow you to atoms," Mox growled. Behind him on the quarterdeck sat several grim-faced men.

Yana gasped. Tycho looked at her questioningly, but her eyes were fixed on the screen.

Diocletia began flipping switches. "Carlo, give me a hand signal when you've got the route to our tanks from Tycho. I'm activating false transponders. Tycho, open a channel on my command. Audio and visual, but restrict the outgoing visual to Mavry's station."

Tycho started to reply, then realized to his horror that he'd lost track of where he was in the navigational calculations.

"Tycho?" Diocletia asked.

"Give me communications," Yana hissed. "I can handle it."

"No, I've got it," Tycho replied.

"You can't do two things at once," Yana said. "And we need that route."

She was right, Tycho realized—without a path to safety they might die, and nothing recorded in the Log would matter. He nodded, and Yana's fingers hammered at her own keys.

"I've got communications, Mom," Yana said.

As brother and sister typed frantically, Mavry dug under his chair and emerged wearing a cracked spacer's cap of stained synthetic leather and oversized goggles that made his eyes look gigantic.

"Open that channel now, Yana," Diocletia said.

Yana nodded and gave her mother a quick thumbs-up. Nobody on the quarterdeck needed to be told to be quiet, not even Huff.

Mavry leaned closer to the camera set in his workstation.

"Easy there, sir, we're receiving transmission," he said in a high-pitched, wheedling voice, scowling and swiveling his head from side to side. "This is the . . ."

nodded, understanding what he was seeing: his parents and Vesuvia had chosen to begin the simulation sometime after the beginning of the battle. He waited for Vesuvia to add the other Jovian ships.

And waited.

There were no other ships, Tycho realized. He had command of a simulated *Kuiper Centurion*, but that was it. All the other Jovian vessels had been destroyed.

Tycho raised his goggles to sneak a quick look at Yana, whose mouth was set in a grim line. Then the yoke wiggled in his hands, telling him that the simulation was beginning.

Tycho survived for fourteen minutes and fifty-three seconds. When his goggles went black, Vesuvia brought up the lights on the quarterdeck. Diocletia and Mavry were sitting at their own stations, where they'd been monitoring the simulations, and turned to regard their children.

"All right," Mavry said. "You all faced the same simulation. Tycho, you made it the longest—nearly fifteen minutes. Tell us what your strategy was."

"I immediately looped back toward the Jovian base on 153 Hilda, angling the *Centurion* to keep my guns aimed at the Earth task force," Tycho said.

"And?" asked Diocletia.

Tycho shook his head.

"And nothing," he said. "I knew I couldn't win outgunned nine to one, so I was playing for time. My hope was that 153 Hilda would send reinforcements."

nervously nearby. Tycho reintroduced himself to Count and Countess Tiamat with a bow, enjoying the sight of his twin sister scowling at him.

"Ah, Master Hashoone," said Count Tiamat. "Your grandfather and I were just reminiscing. Before duty called me home to Ganymede, I spent a few years in the Defense Force. I was gunnery officer on the frigate *Copernican Pilgrimage*—and a pretty good one, I might add! Back then we mostly looked the other way at pirates, but not always. Captain Hashoone and I even took a couple of shots at each other—though fortunately everyone emerged in one piece!"

No sooner had he said this than Count Tiamat seemed to remember that at least half of Huff's body was artificial. He coughed thunderously, clicked his heels together, and continued on like nothing had happened.

"Anyhow, Master Hashoone, allow me to present Captain Holloway, of the JDF Perimeter Patrol," Count Tiamat said.

Holloway gave Tycho the tiniest possible nod.

"Smart lad like you really ought to consider a career in the JDF," Count Tiamat said. "I know I'm biased, but a JDF career can take you anywhere in the solar system, and introduce you to a better element than pirates."

"We're not pirates—we're privateers," Yana objected. "We serve the Jovian Union, just like Captain Holloway does."

Captain Holloway cocked an eyebrow minutely. Huff grunted something and buried his face in a drink.

He shot Diocletia a quick glance. She held up three fingers.

"This is the *Kepler Wanderer*, out of Titania," Mavry said, inserting one finger deep into his nose and rooting around. "We're on a prospecting cruise. Say, we can pay you for any chemical signatures you've recorded. Provided they pan out, of course. I won't pay for bad data, sir!"

"You're a long way from home, *Kepler*," Mox growled. "What are you prospecting for?"

"Why, anything that'll fit in the hold, man!" Mavry said, chuckling. He extracted his finger from his nose, studied it, and flicked it away. "Ain't found nothing but bulk sulfides, though."

Mavry peered into the lens of his camera, getting so close that Tycho knew his face must be wildly distorted on the *Hydra*'s screens.

"Say, you wouldn't be interested in some bulk sulfides, would ya?" Mavry asked. "Find the right buyer on Vesta, you can make a little money."

He rubbed his fingers together, then began scratching at his face, leaving angry red marks. On the screen, the Hashoones saw the dots of the *Hydra*'s pinnaces searching the area. They were small craft, little more than ship's boats, but agile and outfitted with laser cannons and sensors.

"Sorry there, captain," Mavry said, coughing. "The old *Wanderer*'s got mites and fleas and other bugs. We don't mind them, though. Think of them as friends. But next time you stay on Vesta, sir, don't pick the Travelers' Rest. No no no. Oh, what thieves they are at the Travelers' Rest! Why, do you know what they—"

"Shut up, you flea-bitten idiot!" Mox growled. "So you're a rock hunter, are you? I'm quite the enthusiast myself—*gem collector*, you might say. I'm going to send my men aboard your ship to inspect your specimens."

Mavry coughed deeply, then hawked up something and spat it on the deck, leaving a trail of spittle down his chin.

Carlo turned to give Tycho a questioning look. He held up two fingers and kept typing frantically, still calculating the fastest route to the *Comet*'s long-range tanks.

"Are you deaf, sir?" Mavry asked. "Told you, ain't found nothing but bulk sulfides. Terrible stuff, sulfides. Get into the ventilation systems, then into your lungs."

He coughed again, then waved at the camera, wheezing. "You're only welcome if you plan to buy the complete stock, sir. Otherwise, the *Wanderer*'s not taking visitors. We aren't a tourist ship, you know!"

One pinnace had headed to port, the other to starboard, both trying to find the *Comet*.

"Enough jabber," Mox said. "Show yourself and prepare for boarding—or die."

Tycho pumped his fist at Carlo, who whirled back around to his console as their mother nodded.

"Go," she mouthed.

"Die?" demanded Mavry, scraping his tongue with his fingers. "How rude of you. If you have no interest in buying sulfides, sir, this conversation is at an end."

Carlo yanked back on the control yoke and stomped on the throttle, pressing the Hashoones back into their seats as Yana cut the transmission to the *Hydra*. Alarms blared as the *Hydra*'s gunners began firing, sending lances of energy arrowing across space.

"Pinnaces pursuing," Vesuvia said with her usual eerie calm.

"Grigsby, tell the crews to hold fire," Diocletia ordered.

"What?" demanded Huff. The magnets in his metal feet kept him fixed to the deck, motionless, as the ship accelerated. "Mox won't respond to harsh language, Dio!"

"Don't call me that!" barked Diocletia. "I don't want Mox to know we're a privateer, Dad!"

"Mox has his own scanners—and he knows the *Comet* sure as I know the *Hydra*!" Huff said.

"Belay that!" Diocletia said. "Carlo, how long to docking with the tanks?"

"Estimate two minutes on full burn," Carlo said.

"Do it," Diocletia said. "We're not worrying about fuel efficiency today."

"Have a care, Yana," Huff said. "Mox may try to jam our systems."

"No sign of that, Grandfather," Yana replied. "But I'll keep my eyes open."

The *Comet* continued to shake under the onslaught of the *Hydra*'s guns. When a target vessel fled an intercept, every ship involved in the chase burned fuel at an alarming rate, so pursuits tended to be short. If the *Comet* could reach her fuel tanks before the *Hydra* or her pin-naces drew close enough to do real damage, she'd be able to activate the long-range tanks' maneuvering engines and outrun her pursuers.

But if she couldn't . . .

"Are we going to make it?" Yana asked Tycho in a low voice.

"I was just doing the calculations in my head," Tycho replied, then grinned. "Gives you a new appreciation for math!"

Yana shook her head at him in amazement.

"Thanks for taking over communications," Tycho added. "You were right."

"Any time," Yana said.

"Quiet back there!" Diocletia barked as the *Comet* shook again, more violently this time. Tycho tried to remind himself that the *Hydra* was still too far away for her guns to do real damage.

"Carlo, talk to me!" Diocletia said.

"Going fast as I can," Carlo said. "At the current rate of fuel burn—"

"Give me the short version—are we going to make it or not?" Diocletia asked.

"It'll be close," Carlo said. "One minute to docking."

The ship shuddered again. Diocletia activated her microphone.

"Mr. Grigsby, fire at will," she said. "Defend this ship and all who sail on her."

"That we shall, Captain," Grigsby said.

A moment later the *Comet* shook again, but this time it was due to the recoil of her guns. The first volley of shots grew to a continuous roar as Grigsby's crews opened up on the pursuing pirates.

"Arrr!" Huff roared. "We'll blast you clear back to Io, Mox!"

The *Comet* shuddered, there was a shriek of metal, and her nose pitched sideways.

"Pursuers in range," Vesuvia said.

"No kidding," Yana muttered.

Mavry pointed out the forward viewport. The fuel tanks were a bright dot ahead.

"After we dock, what heading do you want?" Tycho asked.

"Anywhere but here," Diocletia said.

The *Comet*'s tanks grew in size, becoming a cluster of dots. But the ship continued to shudder as the pinnaces' cannons hammered away at her.

"Mr. Grigsby?" Diocletia asked.

"Givin' it everything we've got, Captain," Grigsby yelled back over the roar.

"Hang on," warned Carlo. He shoved the control yoke left and the *Comet* slewed that way; then he cut the throttle as the ship shot upward into the fuel tanks' cradle of struts. Something flashed on the screen, and a cheer erupted from belowdecks.

"Got one!" Tycho exulted. One of the pinnaces was retreating the way it had come, wounded by Grigsby's gunners.

The *Comet* jumped and rattled as another explosion jolted her. Then they heard the clank of the hull brackets locking themselves into the tank attachments. The ship shook hard enough to fling them sideways in their restraints.

"Sorry about the bump," Carlo said.

"Stabilizers engaged," Vesuvia said. "Connecting fuel lines."

"Come on, come on, come on!" Tycho urged.

The *Comet* shook again. What could be taking Vesuvia so long?

"Fuel lines connected," Vesuvia said.

Carlo stomped on the throttle, and the acceleration slammed them back in their seats, hard enough to force their eyes closed and drive the air out of their lungs. Even Huff grabbed for the ladder. Tycho grunted, trying to breathe, as the *Comet* rocketed away from her pursuers into the safety of deep space.

The thunder of the guns ceased belowdecks. After a moment the brutal acceleration eased, leaving the Hashoones sitting in stunned silence.

"Carlo, that was good flying," Diocletia said.

"Thank you, Captain," Carlo said with a smile.

Diocletia turned to nod at Yana and Tycho.

"And that was a smooth handoff of duties under fire," she added.

Yana and Tycho exchanged relieved looks.

"Sheesh. See if I try to sell sulfides to that guy again," Mavry said.

Diocletia looked over at her husband, still wearing his goggles and cap.

"You should wear that hat more often, dear," she said with a faint smile. "But only if you stop picking your nose. It's a disgusting habit."

11

RETURN TO CERES

O nce the engineer verified that the *Comet* had taken only minor damage in her encounter with the *Hydra*, Diocletia ordered Carlo to plot a course back to Ceres—their next court date with Judge Quence was just a couple of days away. Besides, she explained, the Jovian Defense Ministry would need time to consider her report of the close encounter with Mox.

As they went about their duties, Tycho noticed that Yana looked preoccupied. After Carlo calculated the

proper course for their trip to Ceres, she asked Vesuvia to
replay the transmission from the *Hydra*.

"Why do you want to look at Thoadbone's ugly mug
again, missy?" asked Huff. "Once is one time too often to
have to see that vacuum-hearted traitor."

"Just watch," Yana said. "Vesuvia, play it back."

Once again Mox was on the main screen, demanding
that the *Comet* submit to boarding by his thugs.

"There!" Yana said. "I know that man."

"We all know Thoadbone Mox," Carlo said with a
snort, though Tycho was pretty sure his brother had gotten his first look at the scarred old pirate at the same
time Tycho and Yana had.

"Not Mox," Yana said, irritated. "Vesuvia, freeze the
image. *That* man."

She pointed to one of the crewers over Mox's left
shoulder, a spacer who struck Tycho as much like any
other, aside from his choice of company.

"Remember him from Ceres?" Yana asked.

"You mean the guy we followed from the courtroom—Suud's aide?" Tycho asked. "Sorry, Yana, but it's
not him."

"Would you wait a second?" Yana asked, tapping at
her mediapad. "Vesuvia, split the screen in two. Leave
the man from the *Hydra* on the left and put this image
from my mediapad on the right."

"Rendering image," Vesuvia said.

A moment later the new image came up on the
screen. It was the picture Yana had snapped of Suud's

aide when she'd pushed Tycho into the Martian spacer. There were two men next to him, who'd also turned to see what had caused the commotion. The man in the middle was the one on the quarterdeck of the *Hydra*.

Mavry whistled.

"I don't think I want to know how you wound up taking a picture of a crewer on Thoadbone Mox's pirate ship," Diocletia said.

"You're right—you don't," Yana said.

Mother and daughter stared at each other for a moment. Then Diocletia sighed.

"Okay, Yana, well observed," Diocletia said. "Now what does it mean?"

"It means Threece Suud is working with Mox," Yana said.

Mavry cocked an eyebrow. "Does it?"

"Okay, someone working with Threece Suud is also working with one of Mox's bridge crew," Yana said. "Is that better?"

"Much," said Mavry.

"It's an interesting connection, isn't it?" asked Yana.

"All they were doing was walking together," said Carlo. "What if they're old friends? Or brothers?"

That seemed ridiculous to Tycho, and he started to say so, but then he stopped. Huff was an old pirate, but during his career he'd come to know Jovian Defense Force officers, judges on Ceres, and nobles from Ganymede. The solar system was a big place, Tycho thought, but human connections could make it feel small.

"If they're friends or brothers, that's even more interesting," Yana told Carlo. "I'm telling you, there's no way it's a coincidence to find one of Suud's aides walking with a member of Mox's bridge crew."

Diocletia cut off Carlo before he could speak.

"We're all tired," she said. "I don't know what it means, and I don't think we're going to figure it out now. The only thing I know for sure is that I don't like it."

The Hashoones hadn't even sat down in Judge Quence's courtroom when Threece Suud came striding over, smiling in a way that showed a lot of very big white teeth and reminded Tycho of ancient Earth predators he'd seen in holo-documentaries. He wasn't wearing his iridescent suit today; instead, he wore a long scarlet coat with tails over a ruffled black shirt.

"Captain Hashoone," he said to Diocletia, taking her hand in both of his and bowing over it. "I'm afraid we got off on the wrong foot last time. It's unfortunate to be adversaries in the courtroom before one is formally introduced."

"And yet that is what we are—adversaries," said Diocletia, jerking her hand out of his.

Suud looked like he hadn't noticed her reaction, turning to Mavry and extending his hand. Mavry ignored it, and after a moment Suud pulled the hand back.

"Mr. Malone," Suud said, giving Mavry a shallower bow than his wife had received.

"It's *First Mate* Malone," Mavry said. "That's quite an outfit, Councilor Suud. You must be the talk of Ceres."

"It's *Secretary* Suud," Suud replied with a frosty smile. "I'm glad you like it. It's zero-gravity fibers, made to order by Hong Kong tailors according to a thousand years of family tradition. I'd be honored to give you their card."

"That's very kind of you, Mr. Suud," Mavry said. "But I'm afraid we're not so formal aboard the *Shadow Comet*."

Suud smiled minutely and extended his hand to Huff, who turned his back with a dismissive grunt. Undeterred, he turned to the younger Hashoones.

"Carlo, Tycho, and Yana," he said. "Your reputations precede you. Your parents must be very proud."

"Don't speak to my children, Suud," Diocletia snapped. "May I remind you that you've accused them of all manner of crimes?"

"It's okay, Mother," Carlo said. "It's an honor to serve as bridge crew aboard the *Comet*, Secretary Suud. Just as it's an honor to do our patriotic duty as privateers in service of the Jovian Union."

He smiled at Suud and offered a very slight bow of his own. Yana grinned.

"Your sense of duty is commendable," Suud said. "But duty is often difficult, of course. As I understand it, you are all competitors for the captaincy. Isn't that the Jovian tradition?"

"That's correct," Carlo said, his eyes wary.

"How awkward," Suud said with a sad smile and wide eyes. "Even without considering the legal ambiguity and moral uncertainty of your profession, it must be a terrible strain to be rivals as well as siblings. Knowing that one of you will be captain, but the other two will see their dreams dashed."

"We're used to it," Carlo said frostily.

"Now look here, you little weasel—" Huff growled. The stump of his forearm swiveled frantically, sensing how badly Huff wanted to shoot somebody.

"A moment, Mr. Hashoone," Suud said, smiling, before turning back to Carlo, Yana, and Tycho. "I am merely concerned for your welfare. I'm sure operating an antique starship is exciting, but what about your futures? On Earth you'd be receiving a first-rate education, one that would prepare you for any number of possible careers."

"Careers?" demanded Huff. "What, train 'em to be bilge-suckin' gum flappers or dead-eyed paper pushers? What lad or lass what's right in the head would pick rottin' in school over the life of a pirate?"

"Privateer," Diocletia said, stepping between her father and Suud. "It's obvious you don't know the first thing about running a starship, Secretary. I'll wager my children know more about mathematics and physics than most Earth children do. What's more—"

The bailiff rapped his staff on the floor and called the court to order. Judge Quence was waddling out of his chambers with his wig on backward. As Quence rearranged his hairpiece properly atop his head, Suud gave the Hashoones a last smile and bow, then offered the same to the Jovian Union officials sitting behind them. He then took his place at the table on his side of the courtroom, next to a glum-looking Soughton.

"I don't like that man," Yana whispered to Tycho as he sat down in front of her at the table with Diocletia.

"Neither do I," Tycho replied. Yana, he saw, was scanning the bureaucrats sitting behind Suud and Soughton.

"Second row, on the aisle," she whispered. "It's the aide we saw with Mox's crewer. No, Tyke, don't look!"

Diocletia gave them both a glower of warning.

"Now then," Judge Quence said. "Before we once again take up the matter of the *Cephalax II* and her alleged diplomatic immunity, I have a question for Secretary Suud."

Suud shot to his feet, the heels of his glossy shoes clicking together. Tycho wondered what expensive orbital factory had made them.

"It would be an honor, Your Honor," Suud said with a deep bow.

"My heart leaps to hear it," Judge Quence said. "It seems another Jovian privateer is on its way to Ceres with a prize seized in deep space. This prize is an Earth-registered freighter carrying a hold full of fourth-degree synthetic fertilizer, captured with one engine unlit and her air scrubbers running at twenty-five percent efficiency."

"Dunno who the lucky privateer is, Quencie, but her captain can have 'er!" burst out Huff.

Judge Quence brought the gavel down so hard that his wig flipped off his head and disappeared behind him.

"Sorry, Quen—Your Honor," Huff said sheepishly as

Quence and the bailiff hunted behind the podium for the escaped wig. Judge Quence reappeared a moment later, red-faced but with his wig back in place.

"Now then," Quence said. "What particularly interests me, Secretary Suud, is that in addition to her rather dull cargo and lengthy list of inspection violations, this freighter was carrying an Earth diplomat—one who only recently joined the diplomatic service. What might you know about all this, Secretary Suud?"

Judge Quence folded his hands and looked serenely out at Suud.

If Suud was worried, though, he didn't show it. He stepped in front of the table and turned to the courtroom with a wide smile, as if nothing would make him happier than to discuss diplomatic credentialing with those attending a session of the Ceres Admiralty Court.

"Your Honor, Earth desires close, cordial relationships with all its former colonies, whatever the current regrettable state of affairs between them," Suud said. "Achieving that outcome is the principal goal of all members of the diplomatic corps."

"I wasn't looking for an appreciation of Earth's diplomats, fine people though they surely are," Judge Quence said. "What I'd like to know is why they're increasingly turning up on old scows."

Tycho's eyes widened. He leaned over to say something to Diocletia. She waved him away, but he shook his head insistently.

"What?" Diocletia demanded in a whisper.

Judge Quence gave Diocletia a warning glance but decided her offense wasn't grave enough for the gavel.

"Your Honor, in pursuing the goal of interplanetary friendship, occasionally the fastest way for diplomats to travel is aboard merchant ships registered with Earth," Suud told the judge. "The diplomatic corps has struck arrangements . . ."

As Suud droned on, Tycho hurriedly told his mother what Countess Tiamat had said back at the party above Ganymede, about Earth registering hundreds of new diplomats.

Diocletia frowned at Tycho.

"You're sure that's what she said?" she asked.

Tycho nodded.

Judge Quence gave the gavel a short, sharp rap.

"Captain Hashoone, is this really the most appropriate time to be instructing one of your children?" he asked.

"I beg your pardon, Your Honor," Diocletia said. "Tycho and I required a brief consultation. May I ask Secretary Suud a question?"

"That would obviously be inappropriate," Suud snapped.

"By all means, Captain Hashoone," Judge Quence said with a smile.

"Thank you, Your Honor," Diocletia said. "Secretary Suud, how many Earth diplomats are traveling aboard merchant ships at the moment?"

"Your interest in the work of His Majesty's diplomatic

corps is commendable, Captain Hashoone," Suud said. "It would be most appropriate for an answer to such inquiries to come from—"

BAM! went the gavel.

"Answer the question, Secretary Suud," Judge Quence barked.

Suud frowned and crouched in the aisle, speaking briefly to a female aide with a mediapad. He nodded and sat in his chair, looking down at his hands for a moment.

"Well?" Judge Quence asked.

"Currently there are four hundred and twelve," Suud said.

Judge Quence's eyebrows shot upward. Carlo, Yana, and Tycho looked at one another. The Jovians behind them muttered in astonishment until Judge Quence gaveled the courtroom into silence.

"And how many merchant ships flying the flag of Earth are currently carrying cargoes in the solar system?" Diocletia asked.

"There is absolutely no way I am sharing such sensitive information with a known pirate!" Suud sputtered.

Diocletia just smiled.

"Never mind. I've got a pretty good guess," she said. "It's four hundred and twelve, isn't it?"

Suud didn't say anything, but he didn't need to—his grimace was answer enough.

"I think it's obvious what's going on here, Your Honor," Diocletia said. "Earth is labeling regular crewers or passengers as diplomats, to prevent the lawful practice of privateering."

Suud leaped to his feet.

"Your Honor, calling privateering lawful is a miscarriage of justice, one that Earth has suffered for far too long," he said.

Suud turned to glare at the Hashoones and the Jovian Union officials seated behind them. He was no longer making the slightest effort to appear friendly.

"Let me remind the court that Earth has *never* resorted to the illegal practice of privateering, despite the fact that technically we remain at war," Suud said. "Given our far greater population and economic power, I'd ask my Jovian friends to consider the effect on their trade if His Majesty were to change his mind about that policy."

Yana poked Tycho in the shoulder. He glanced over at Suud's side of the room and saw that the mustachioed man they'd followed was smiling nastily to himself.

"Your Honor, is privateering now on trial?" Diocletia demanded.

"No, it is not," Judge Quence said, gavel raised threateningly. "As Secretary Suud knows perfectly well. We shall stick to the subject at hand."

"Very well," Suud said. "Captain Hashoone's accusations are dramatic, but beside the point. As I'm sure Your Honor is aware, nothing in space law restricts who can or cannot be a diplomat."

"What about basic fairness?" burst out Tycho. "I don't know anything about laws, Your Honor, but isn't it wrong to twist them up so they mean something they're not supposed to?"

"Aye to that," growled Huff. "Well said, Tyke."

BAM! went Judge Quence's gavel.

"That will do, Master Hashoone," he said.

"Your Honor, I must insist—" said Suud.

BAM!

Suud contented himself with glaring at Diocletia, who glared back.

"Your Honor, I request that a registry of diplomats currently serving aboard Earth's merchant ships be entered into the record," Diocletia said.

That sent Suud to his feet again, face flushed.

"This is outrageous!" he sputtered. "Surely Your Honor will not allow this court to aid and abet future acts of piracy by Captain Hashoone and her brood!"

"Come now, Secretary Suud," Diocletia said. "I'm not asking you for what ships your diplomats are traveling on—just their names and backgrounds. I believe that's public information, is it not? And since you yourself have just told us there are no restrictions on who gets to be a diplomat, why the objection?"

Judge Quence raised his eyebrows under his wig. Threece Suud, Tycho noticed, was turning an alarming shade of purple. But then he pressed his hands together and bent his head down so that his chin was practically touching his breastbone. When he lifted his head, he was smiling serenely once more.

"Very well," Suud said, turning to gesture to a female

aide. "We shall file it within the hour, Your Honor, if only to put an end to Captain Hashoone's theatrical sideshow and demonstrate that Earth has nothing to hide in this matter."

"Thank you, Secretary Suud," Judge Quence said, then steepled his fingers and frowned.

"I dislike cases that get further and further from resolution," he said after a moment, "but this seems to be one of them. I need to think about it more. Until I reach some conclusion, this court stands adjourned."

demanded. "It's obvious he's up to something, the low-bred Earth snake!"

"You've been hanging around Grandfather too much—you're starting to talk like him," Tycho said with a grin. "Shh, here comes Suud."

Suud's scarlet outfit looked even more ridiculous surrounded by the drab coveralls and jumpsuits of the spacers, workers, and merchants in the crowded tunnels. Suud, still looking furious, spoke briefly with a couple of his aides—including the man with the mustache—before heading left as Tycho and Yana bent their heads together, trying not to be noticed.

The man with the mustache headed right. Yana and Tycho followed, careful to keep at least five or six people between themselves and their quarry. They stayed with him through the corridors and pressure domes, passing the chandler's depot where Yana had spotted him last time and the point where they'd had to turn back. A couple of minutes later, he stopped outside a scuzzy-looking spacer bar and talked briefly into his headset, while Yana and Tycho peeked out at him from beside a grimy air-filtration pump. Then he walked into the bar.

"Let's go inside," Yana said.

"He'll see us," Tycho said.

"No, he won't," Yana said. "It's lunchtime—it'll be crowded. Come on, Tyke!"

"All right," Tycho said. "Take it easy."

The door to the bar was plain and gray, like nearly every other one on Ceres, but the owner had surrounded it with loops of flexible lighting and flashing signs for various intoxicants. About half of the signs were damaged or dark.

Yana reached for the button to open the door, but a meaty hand grabbed her wrist before her finger could get there. The hand belonged to a huge, rough-looking man in a dirty jumpsuit, an unlit cheroot clenched in his yellow teeth.

"No kids," the man grunted. Annoyed, Yana yanked her arm out of his grip.

"We just want some jump-pop," Yana said. "They have orange. That's the best flavor, don't you think?"

"No kids," the man said again.

"But our parents told us to meet them here," Yana said. "They're navigators on the *Tiamat's Pride*, out of Ganymede. You know the ship, right?"

"Never heard of it," the bouncer said. "No kids. Wait outside."

"But they told us to meet them *inside*," Yana said. "We'll get in trouble!"

"You got communicators," the bouncer pointed out.

"But—"

The bouncer crossed his arms and set his feet wide apart.

"No kids," he grunted. "I ain't gonna say it again, missy."

"Come on," Tycho said, and yanked on his sister's sleeve. She resisted momentarily, and he wondered if he'd have to drag her off.

"The business end of a blaster cannon would do wonders for your manners," Yana told the bouncer, who shrugged. She shot him a last furious look and retreated down the passageway, stopping on the far side of the air-filtration pump.

"What do we do now?" Tycho asked.

"We wait," Yana said firmly. "It's not like he lives there—he has to come out eventually."

"All right," Tycho said, settling himself against the wall of the passage, separated from the bar's bouncer—now puffing contently on his cheroot—by Ceres's endless parade of passing spacers, miners, and workers. Within a few minutes Yana was sighing and fidgeting and Tycho's stomach was growling.

Something pinged inside Yana's bag. She pulled out her mediapad and nodded.

"What is it?" Tycho asked.

"Suud filed his list of diplomats serving aboard merchant ships," Yana said, finger flicking across the screen.

"Is Soughton on it?" Tycho asked, leaning over to take a look.

"I'll check. You keep your eye on the door," Yana said. "Hmm, no Soughton. That's weird."

"No, it isn't," Tycho realized. "He's probably not aboard a ship—I bet Suud told him to cool his heels here on Ceres until Judge Quence reaches his decision."

"There are other diplomats who also work for Carnegie-Frick Ventures, though," Yana said. "Here's one. And another. And another. They're all recently accredited diplomats, just like him."

Tycho peered over her shoulder.

"But look at all these other companies who have diplomats working for them," he said. "What's Englert and Brout Consultants? Look, the guy who used to work there has been in the service for only six weeks. Same with these two from Franklin-Bundy Space Services, whatever that is."

"Tyke, look!" Yana said.

Tycho glanced up and saw Suud's aide come out of the bar, along with a skinny man with red hair buzzed close to his skull and a barrel-chested bald man. The bald man had fingers studded with rings, and glowing tattoos spiraled up his arms, winking on and off according to some internal clock.

The bouncer, Tycho noticed, moved several steps away, taking a sudden interest in the glowing tip of his cheroot.

Yana's hand closed hard around her brother's wrist.

"The red-haired man," she whispered, eyes wide. "He's the other one from my photo! He was the guy with Suud's aide and Mox's crewer!"

Tycho peered at the red-haired man.

"Are you sure?" he asked.

"I was right last time, wasn't I?" Yana said, fumbling with her mediapad. "We have to figure out who he is. Let me get another photo."

"Don't!" Tycho said. "If one of them sees you, we're cooked!"

Yana started to argue, but just then the bouncer's eyes flicked over to them. Tycho and Yana held their breath as the man studied them for a moment, then dismissed them and continued studying the passersby.

Suud's aide shook the bald man's hand and nodded to the red-haired man, who dug in his pocket and handed the bald man a currency chip. The bald man flipped it in the air and caught it, grinning to show a mouthful of silver teeth filed into points. Suud's aide went back inside the bar while the bald man turned and walked in the Hashoones' direction, swaying slightly.

Tycho turned his back and stepped in front of his sister, hoping the bald man wouldn't notice them. People pushed past them, muttering complaints. A moment later, Yana was striding down the corridor in the other direction.

"He didn't see us," she said over her shoulder. "Hurry up, Tyke, Mr. Red's getting away!"

Tycho rushed after his sister, offering hasty apologies to the gangs of spacers she had just pushed past. The corridor led into a pressure dome filled with secondhand equipment shops, broken up by ramshackle eateries and a bank of public communications booths. They caught sight of the red-haired man on the other side of the dome, beyond a gaggle of prospectors.

"We should have split up," Yana said. "You could have followed the bald pirate while I went after Mr. Red."

"*If* the bald guy's a pirate," Tycho muttered. "Maybe the red-haired man just owed him money. Maybe they were settling a bet."

"Now you sound like Carlo," Yana snorted. "The last time we saw Mr. Red and Suud's aide walking around Ceres, one of their buddies turned up on the quarterdeck of a pirate ship. And that bald guy sure looked like he belongs on one."

Tycho and Yana followed the red-haired man down another corridor, through another dome, and into yet another passageway. Halfway down that corridor, he stopped in front of a door, taking an identification card out of his pocket. He ran it through a reader beside the door, which slid aside to let him in.

"Yana, wait a minute!" Tycho said, catching up with his sister as she hurried down the corridor. "We don't know what's in there. What if we run right into him on the other side?"

Yana frowned and kicked at the molded rock of the corridor wall.

"See if you can get a map view of where we are," Tycho said. "And if there's any listing for the address."

Yana nodded and got out her mediapad, tapping at its surface.

"Here's the map view," Yana said, tilting the mediapad so Tycho could see it. The corridor they were in was a spoke connecting the hubs of pressure domes. On the other side of the mysterious door, they could see, was a cluster of smaller domes.

Yana's fingers danced over the mediapad's keys.

"The address is listed, but there's no information about what's there," she said.

"That's no surprise. Plenty of organizations on Ceres don't want people looking into their business," Tycho said.

"So there's no way to find out," Yana grumbled.

"Well, there's *one* way," Tycho said, looking down the passageway. "Be ready to look like dumb kids who are lost."

"Isn't that pretty much what we are?" Yana asked.

"I hope not," Tycho said. "Come on."

The door was unmarked, with a glowing white button, a card reader, a speaker grille beside it, and a security camera above.

"I've got an idea," Tycho said, pulling a currency chip out of one of his pockets. "Follow my lead, okay?"

He pushed the button beside the door. They heard a low buzz and the door slid into the wall. Tycho and Yana found themselves in a waiting room lit by dim, flickering overhead lights. A few plastic chairs faced a desk, behind which sat a pinch-faced woman with suspicious eyes and a grimace that looked permanent.

"Can I help you?" she asked, her tone making it clear that there were few things she'd like to do less.

"You sure can, thanks," Tycho said brightly. "What's the name of this office?"

"A number of companies have offices here," the woman said.

"I see," Tycho said. "The man who just came in, the one with the red hair—we have something for him."

"And what would that be?" the woman asked.

"I'm sorry, that's personal," Tycho said, taking a marking stylus from his pocket. "Say, could I borrow an envelope?"

"Not unless I know what this is regarding," the woman said.

"Well, he dropped this," Tycho said, holding up the currency chip. "We don't know how much is on it."

The woman behind the desk looked from the chip to Tycho and Yana, then smiled. Somehow it made her seem even less friendly.

"I'll make sure it gets to him," she said, sticking out her hand.

"We'd prefer to give it to him personally," Tycho said.

"Are you saying you don't trust me?" the woman asked.

Yana stepped forward, her face contorted in a sneer borrowed from a Ceres dome urchin.

"We found the chip, so we get the reward!" she said, then shook her fist.

Tycho thought that last bit bordered on overacting, but he played his part, holding up a hand to stop his sister.

"C'mon, sis, that's not fair," he said. "Grandpa always said we should assume the best of people. Remember?"

Yana grumbled something under her breath.

"You should listen to your brother," said the woman behind the desk, her eyes on the chip in Tycho's hand.

"We just want the man who dropped this to know who found it for him," Tycho said, trying to sound small and despairing.

"I already told you that I'll tell him," the woman behind the desk said, eyes still on the chip. "Come back tomorrow and I'll give you your reward—if there is one."

Tycho looked doubtful, and the woman sighed, exasperated.

"What did you expect? Did you think he'd put a couple of half-grown dome rats like you on the jobs list?"

Yana's eyes went wide. Alarmed, Tycho kicked her in the ankle and looked pleadingly at the woman, acting as if he hadn't heard the scorn in her voice.

"Oh, ma'am, a job would be such a big help . . . you can't even imagine," he said.

The woman behind the desk laughed.

"You're a little young for that line of work," she said, and held out her hand, palm up. "Now come on. Give me the chip."

"We're not giving that chip to anybody except the man who dropped it!" Yana exclaimed.

The woman behind the desk looked from one Hashoone to the other.

"My sister's right," Tycho said, putting the chip back in his pocket. "I hate to doubt you, ma'am, but these are hard times. Could you call him, please?"

The woman behind the desk glowered at them for a moment, then activated her headset and tapped at her mediapad.

"Is Mr. Hindman available?" she asked, then instantly began talking again. "No? How long? Really? Okay. No, no message."

She shut down her headset and smiled thinly at Tycho and Yana.

"He's in meetings all day," she said. "So unless you want to wait . . ."

Tycho and Yana looked at each other.

"I guess we have no choice but to wait," Yana said, sounding reluctant.

"No, it's fine, sis," Tycho said, narrowing his eyes at Yana and hoping she'd catch the hint. "Could I borrow that envelope now, ma'am? And maybe a piece of scrap?"

"But—" said Yana.

"We can't wait all day," Tycho said, emphasizing each word. Yana fluttered her hands, clearly annoyed with him, but didn't argue further.

The woman handed over an envelope and a piece of paper, both of which had been recycled so many times they were a dingy beige. Tycho scrawled something on the note with his stylus, popped it in the envelope along with the chip, sealed the envelope, and wrote HINDMAN across the front. The woman's eyes, he saw, were fixed on the envelope.

"I'm sorry, I can never spell his firm's name right," Tycho said casually, fighting the urge to hold his breath.

"It's just like it sounds," the woman said quizzically. "S-M-I-T-H. Smith Maritime."

Yana looked away, face turning red, and put her hand over her mouth.

"She thinks I'm an idiot," Tycho said hurriedly. "I always want to spell 'Smith' with a Y, for some reason."

He held up the envelope, which the woman all but snatched out of his hand and immediately put in a drawer.

"Please make sure Mr. Hindman gets that," Tycho said.

"Oh, I will. Don't you kids worry," the woman said. "Have a nice day."

Tycho and Yana slapped hands in the corridor, not caring about the security camera. Tycho was sure the woman behind the desk was already tossing the envelope and note in the recycling and pocketing the chip. Even if she did realize she'd been conned, the last thing she'd do was tell the mysterious Mr. Hindman of Smith Maritime what had happened.

"I didn't think you knew what you were doing back there, Tyke, but that was beautiful," Yana said as they reentered the pressure dome full of equipment shops.

"Thanks . . . I think," Tycho said, then grinned. "I wish I could see her face when she finds out that chip barely has enough on it for a carton of jump-pop."

"Me too," Yana said. "But now I want to know what Smith Maritime is."

"And who Hindman is," Tycho said.

Yana took out her mediapad and plopped down at a rickety table outside a café while Tycho bought a jump-pop and some nutrient squares to keep the owner from shooing them away.

"The public listing doesn't tell us much," Yana said, showing him the result of her search. "Services for interplanetary cargo transportation, offices on Ceres and Vesta."

"Go back to Suud's list of current diplomats," Tycho suggested, biting off the corner of a square. "See if any of them work for Smith Maritime."

Yana brightened and nodded, fingers flying over her mediapad as she called up the list of current diplomats.

"Yes!" she said, smiling at Tycho. "Here's one who does. And here's another."

"What about Hindman? Is he on the list?" Tycho asked, trying to keep the growing excitement out of his voice.

"You're drinking all the jump-pop," Yana complained.

"Forget the stupid jump-pop!" Tycho said. "Is Hindman a diplomat or not?"

"Let me see," Yana said, fingers tapping eagerly. But then her shoulders sagged. "No, he isn't."

"You're sure?" Tycho asked. He could feel the disappointment like a weight in his chest.

"Positive," Yana said.

"Okay," Tycho said. "Give me a moment."

His brain felt like it was spinning. He and Yana were on the right track—he knew it. They'd discovered something important, something that might explain the strange events on Ceres and why Earth suddenly had so many diplomats. A solution to their court case would look awfully good in the Log, but what was that solution?

Tycho tried to think. There was Suud's mustachioed aide, and the redheaded Hindman, and the pirate from the *Hydra*, and the bald man, and the list of diplomats, and the companies they used to work for, and they were all connected somehow. But how?

"While you stare into space, I'm gonna get a jump-pop of my own," Yana said, pulling a currency chip from her pocket and getting to her feet.

Tycho glanced at the chip held in Yana's fingertips, then grabbed his sister's arm.

"Hey!" she protested.

"Hindman isn't a diplomat," Tycho said, tapping the currency chip. "He's the guy who hires them."

Yana sank back down in her chair.

"Go on," she said.

"We saw Hindman walking with Suud's aide and a bunch of scuzzy-looking spacers—one of whom is part of Mox's crew," Tycho said. "Today we saw him pay the bald guy after Suud's aide was done talking with him. The woman at Smith Maritime talked about a jobs list, and now we see that several of the new diplomats work for Smith Maritime. It all adds up."

Yana nodded. "That's right. But what about all these other companies? Why would they all hire people just so they can become Earth diplomats?"

"Look up Carnegie-Frick—Soughton's company," Tycho said. "See if there's a public listing."

He nibbled at a nutrient square while Yana tapped and scrolled. The square was stale.

"Carnegie-Frick, security consultants to the space-transportation industry," Yana said. "Offices on Earth, the Moon, and Mars."

"Security consultants?" Tycho asked, drumming his fingers on the table. "Sounds to me like a nicer name for what Grandpa called leg breakers."

"It also sounds pretty much the same as the listing for Smith Maritime," Yana said.

"You're right, it does," Tycho said. "Go back to the list of diplomats. Look and see if there are public listings for the other companies they work for."

Englert and Brout were interplanetary shipping consultants, with offices on Mars and in the asteroid belt. Franklin-Bundy specialized in cargo security, and their offices were on the Moon. The next name they tried belonged to consultants based on the asteroid 221 Eos. Tycho pictured a succession of dreary waiting rooms outside drab offices that were way stations for men and women who spent their lives in space.

"Let's call one of them and see what we can figure out," suggested Yana. "We'll use a public comm so they can't track it."

Tycho took the carton of jump-pop, and they squeezed into the half booth of an unoccupied public communicator, its rusty exterior sporting dents and graffiti.

"Try Carnegie-Frick," Tycho said. "Remember to blank the screen."

"I know how to use a comm, Tyke," Yana replied, copying the contact information from her mediapad.

"You do the talking. You're on a roll today."

Carnegie-Frick's logo appeared on the comm's screen, and a chime sounded.

"Welcome to Carnegie-Frick," said a cultured female voice. The intonation was perfectly regular—a giveaway that this was an artificial intelligence, not a person. "How may I direct you?"

"Um, we run a small family shipping company out of Ceres," Tycho said. "We're wondering what services you offer."

"I'm sorry, Carnegie-Frick is limited to institutional customers," the smooth female voice said. "Good-bye."

The screen went black.

"Well, that was rude," Yana said.

"Try Englert and Brout," Tycho said.

The same cool, artificial female voice answered.

"Um, is this Englert and Brout?" asked Tycho, startled.

"It is," the artificial voice said. "How may I direct you?"

"It's about my family's interplanetary shipping company, out of . . . um, Mars," Tycho said. "I'm interested in a services contract with your company."

"I'm sorry, Englert and Brout is limited to institutional customers," the voice said. "Good-bye."

"That was weird," Tycho said, but Yana shrugged.

"They just use the same artificial-intelligence avatar. So what?" she said.

"They also have the exact same message," Tycho said. "Let's try Smith Maritime."

"And talk to that harpy again?" Yana asked. "She must know we tricked her by now."

"I bet she won't be the one answering the call," Tycho said. "Would you want her talking to customers on the comm?"

"Good point," Yana said.

"Welcome to Smith Maritime," said a now-familiar artificial female voice. "How may I direct you?"

"I represent an institutional shipping company," Tycho said. "We're looking to see if your services meet our needs."

"I'm sorry, Smith Maritime is not taking new customers at this time," the voice said. "Good-bye."

"Huh," Tycho said.

"Move on to the next one?" Yana asked.

"No," Tycho said. "Try Carnegie-Frick again."

Yana looked doubtful but reentered the contact information. The Carnegie-Frick logo materialized, and the chime sounded.

"Welcome to Carnegie-Frick," the voice said. "How may I direct you?"

"My firm specializes in artificial-intelligence programs," Tycho said. "We'd like to discuss your customer-service needs with the appropriate person."

"All such inquiries should be directed to GlobalRex Reinsurance, a subsidiary of the GlobalRex Corporation," the cool voice recited. "Good-bye."

Tycho nodded.

"Now Englert and Brout," he said.

"Let me try it this time," Yana said, dialing and listening to the artificial intelligence's greeting.

"I run a company that makes artificial-intelligence programs," she said. "We'd like to discuss your customer-service needs with the appropriate person."

"All such inquiries should be directed—" the voice began.

"—to GlobalRex Reinsurance," Tycho and Yana finished, nodding at each other.

"They're all the same company," Yana said. "All of Threece Suud's fake diplomats were hired by the same place—and GlobalRex has gone to a lot of trouble to keep people from figuring that out."

"Except we just did," Tycho said with a grin.

"So what are they so determined to hide?" Yana asked.

"Well, we know Earth is trying to stop privateering by putting fake diplomats on all their merchant ships, right?"

"Right," Yana said.

"And we know—or at least we're pretty sure—that those diplomats are just thugs like Soughton, hired by men like Hindman to work for GlobalRex's fake companies," Tycho said.

"Right again," Yana said. "Which is wrong. It has to be."

"I agree it's wrong," Tycho said. "But is it *illegal*?"

"Well, forget about the diplomats. Hindman and Suud's aide were with the pirate from Mox's ship—that sure points to something illegal," Yana said. "And the bald man outside the bar . . . is he a diplomat, or a pirate?"

"Well, he sure looks—" Tycho began, then jumped to his feet and grinned at his sister.

"I've got it!" he said. "Remember Grandfather said those leg breakers—guys like Soughton—were half pirate themselves? Well, men like Hindman find them, and Suud's aide interviews them and approves them. Some of them become Earth's phony diplomats, working for companies that are all really GlobalRex. But others become crewers for pirates like Mox."

Yana leaned forward, eyes widening.

"GlobalRex doesn't want anyone to figure it out, and Suud has arranged things so he never has to know about it," Tycho said. "His aide handles it. That way Suud stays clean."

"That filthy bilge rat," Yana said.

Tycho nodded.

"I should have been listening to Grandfather from the beginning," he said. "Back on Ganymede he said some folks think it's honorable to steal with words and computers, but not with cannons. He said they think they're clean because they don't know the people who do the dirty work. They say we privateers are the ones causing the war with Earth, when they're fighting too— and twice as dirty. And it all points back to one person."

"Threece Suud," Yana said.

"Threece Suud," Tycho agreed.

13

JUPITER'S TRAP

The Jovian Union maintained a sprawling warren of offices connected to one of Ceres's larger pressure domes. Tycho and Yana found the rest of their family there, discussing the finer points of space law with a pair of Jovian officials.

"Can't this wait?" asked a weary-looking Diocletia.

"I don't think it can," Mavry said. "These two look like they're going to blow a hatch seal."

"We are," Yana said. "We know what Suud is doing."

12

MR. RED

Yana had already told Diocletia that she and Tycho were going to follow Suud's aide again, and their mother hadn't argued, only insisted that they be careful. The two youngest Hashoones huddled against the wall of the corridor outside the admiralty court, watching and waiting for their quarry as officials, privateers, and bureaucrats made their way out of the crowded courtroom.

"Did you see the way Suud's aide was smiling?" Yana

"And what's that?" asked Mavry.

"I figured it out," Tycho said. "Suud—"

"Wait a second, you only figured it out because I noticed—" Yana began.

"Stop," Diocletia said. "You can argue about who gets the credit after we decide whether there's something worth getting credit for. Tycho, go ahead."

Tycho decided to explain it like he was writing an essay for Vesuvia to grade. *This is what happened. This is what we think it means. This is the evidence.* He must have done a good job, because Yana didn't interrupt him, and when he was halfway through, the other Hashoones began exchanging wary glances.

"It's circumstantial evidence, but it's a lot of circumstantial evidence," one of the Jovian officials said. "And it fits pretty well with things the Securitat has been seeing—the surge in new diplomats, the increase in pirate activity, the disappearance of Jovian ships."

"So what do we do about it?" Mavry asked.

"I think we'd better talk to the defense minister," the Jovian official said.

A couple of hours later Tycho and Yana found themselves sitting in front of a secure communications link, speaking with the Jovian Union's defense minister and a table of hard-eyed Securitat analysts and aides. Tycho and Yana explained what they'd seen and what they'd discovered—with Yana showing the two pictures from her mediapad—then waited impatiently for their transmission to cross the vast distance between Ceres and Jupiter and for the defense minister's answering transmission to return.

The defense minister thanked them solemnly and said he'd be back in touch. That didn't happen until the next day, though, during a meeting that neither the Hashoone kids nor Huff were invited to. When Diocletia and Mavry emerged from the meeting, they both looked grim.

"What's the matter, Mom?" Yana asked. "Didn't they believe us?"

"They do," Diocletia said. "Let's discuss this in private."

They borrowed a small, stale-smelling conference room and sat down, Huff squeezing his bulk between the table and the wall.

"We've been asked to assist the Jovian Defense Force once again," Diocletia said. "The Securitat agrees Earth is using fake diplomats to evade our privateers while recruiting pirates to damage our commerce."

"Why would Earth need to recruit pirates?" Carlo asked. "Can't they just hire the existing ones?"

"Ain't enough of us out there anymore to do any real harm—it's mostly dead enders like Mox," Huff said, then grinned. "Imagine spacers findin' work as pirates—and right here on Ceres, too! I feared them days were at an end."

Diocletia looked sharply at her father.

"The people hiring pirates are our sworn enemies, Dad," she said.

"Was just about to say as much," Huff muttered. "'Tis a terrible thing, of course."

"Anyway, the question is how to prove it," Diocletia said. "Suud and his bureaucrats are too smart to get caught with their hands dirty, so the pirates are the weak point. Based on our sensor data, the JDF has attributed four recent pirate attacks to the *Hydra*—all on Jovian vessels whose last port of call was Ceres. Mox's ship logs might have a record of Suud's scheme . . . or maybe the pirate from Yana's photo could be made to confess."

"But how are we going to get at Mox's logs?" Yana asked. "Or get the pirate to admit anything?"

"By capturing the *Hydra*," Diocletia said.

Everyone was silent for a moment.

"Arrr," said Huff. "The *Hydra* ain't yer typical prize. You want ol' Thoadbone's ship, yer gonna have to take her at cannonpoint."

"That's the plan," Diocletia said. "The JDF has requisitioned a cargo hauler called the *Vesta Runner* that's been stuck here waiting for a bulk shipment to clear customs on Mars. Her hold is big enough for us and another privateer. We sneak our ships inside the hold; then someone makes the rounds here on Ceres, pretending to be part of the hauler's crew and running his mouth talking about valuable cargo. Then we fly off to the Cybeles, where hopefully Mox is waiting."

Carlo shook his head.

"Has anyone in the history of interplanetary travel ever started a cruise hoping Thoadbone Mox is waiting at the other end?" he asked.

"Probably not," Diocletia said. "That's the plan, though."

"And you said yes?" Yana asked.

"I haven't said anything yet," Diocletia said. "I told the defense minister we had to talk it over as a bridge crew and as a family."

"What's to discuss?" Carlo asked. "You're the captain. Your word is law."

"Yes, it is," Diocletia said. "But this isn't normal privateering, to say the least, and I know some of you were against the last trip we took to the Cybeles. So we'll put it to a vote. Before we do that, does anyone have an argument to make for or against?"

"I do," Yana said.

"Okay, let's hear it," Diocletia said.

"We already nearly got killed out there helping out the JDF," Yana said. "Now they want us to go back?"

"What are you, scared?" asked Carlo, leaning forward to grin at Yana.

"Belay that," Diocletia ordered. "If you're not scared going up against Mox, I don't want you on my crew, because you're going to get us killed."

Carlo drew himself back and folded his arms, angry spots of color in his cheeks.

"I'm not scared," Yana said, glaring at her older brother. "I'm also not a fool. We don't—"

"Belay that too," Diocletia said. "Go on, Yana. More civilly this time."

"We don't do favors for bullies and blackmailers," Yana said. "If they want us to go back out there, they should do more than guarantee our letter of marque— they should pay us."

"Amen to that," growled Huff. "Wisdom from the mouths of babes, that is. If a half-grown girlie can see what's right, surely the rest of you can too."

"Not quite the way I would have put it, but thanks, Grandfather," Yana said.

"Yer welcome," Huff said with a smile.

"Anybody want to make the counterargument?" Diocletia asked.

"I will," Carlo said. "We're Jovians. Those people Mox is capturing out there are our fellow Jovians, and their cargoes are Jovian cargoes. We're privateers, yes. But that means we fight for the Jovian Union. And this is our chance to prove it—to show all those silly, stuck-up people on Ganymede who we are and what we can do."

Diocletia smiled. "Let's vote, then. We'll go around the table. Dad, do we help or not?"

"No," Huff said, folding his arms.

"All right," Diocletia said. "I vote yes. I already spoke with Carina. She may not be flying with us, but this is the family business, so she gets a vote. Which was no. Mavry?"

"Yes," Mavry said.

"I vote yes," Carlo said.

"If they wanted us to go, they should have paid us," Yana said. "I vote no."

"Well then," Diocletia said. "It's three to three. Tycho? You have the deciding vote."

All eyes turned to Tycho, who swallowed and blew out his breath in a long, slow exhalation.

"It's our fellow Jovians out there," he said. "On the other hand, I don't like being pushed around by the people we're supposed to be helping. That isn't right."

"It's a simple question, Tycho," Carlo said. "Yes or no?"

"I don't think it's a simple question at all," Mavry said. "Go on, Tycho."

"I don't like the way the JDF has treated us," Tycho continued. "But what Threece Suud and GlobalRex are doing is worse. Earth has so many more people, so much more money, so many more ships, and now they're hiring pirates to kidnap our people? While claiming they're better than us because they don't believe in privateering?"

Tycho folded his arms.

"That's not right," he said. "And I want to make them pay for it. I vote yes."

14

HUNT FOR THE *HYDRA*

hate being cooped up in here," Yana said, and not for the first time.

They were back in the Cybeles, but this time the *Comet* was inside the cargo bay of the *Vesta Runner*, next to another privateer, the *Ironhawk*. At a command from the *Vesta Runner*'s captain, the massive doors of her cargo bay would swing open and the two privateers would emerge from hiding, ready to engage Thoadbone Mox's ship. Until then, though, the *Comet*'s crew was stuck waiting, annoyed with the *Runner*'s poky pace and her weak sensors.

"It's been four days already—I don't think I can take another one," Yana said.

"We could run another boarding simulation," Tycho suggested. They'd been through more than a dozen, trying to make everything from selecting their gear to clearing corridors while under fire feel familiar.

Yana just groaned and shook her head.

"We all hate being cooped up in here," Carlo said. "The difference is the rest of us don't keep talking about it."

"I'll say what I want—" Yana began hotly, before Diocletia whirled around in the captain's chair with a warning look that silenced both of them.

Huff chuckled, clanking forward to smack Yana on the shoulder with his forearm blaster cannon. Tycho knew it was meant to be a reassuring gesture, but Yana winced and grabbed at her shoulder.

"The pirating life's always this way, lass," Huff said. "Days of waiting, interrupted by minutes of terror."

"Please do not engage that weapon in close proximity to a child," Vesuvia chirped.

"It's not engaged, you half-witted addin' machine," Huff growled.

"Quit calling me a child, Vesuvia!" Yana yelled.

"'Engaged' refers to operational status," Vesuvia said. "If your weapon is not operational, its indicators are faulty and should be repaired."

"I'm twelve years old and a midshipman," Yana protested.

"You want faulty?" Huff asked. "What if I engage this blaster cannon in yer cognitive module, you cheeky tangle of—"

Diocletia turned, eyes blazing.

"Belay that!" she yelled.

Yana and Huff looked at each other.

"Belay what?" Yana asked.

"Belay everything!" Diocletia said. "Honestly, Thoadbone Mox shooting at us would be better than listening to the lot of you!"

"Avast, Dio," Huff muttered in an uncharacteristically small voice. "'Tis bad luck to say that."

Tycho just shook his head. This flying slow and half blind was making them all stir crazy. On top of that, he thought, there was no guarantee Mox would even show up.

They'd done their best to set the trap, sending Carlo and a young crewer from the *Ironhawk* around Ceres's bars and food shacks, wearing borrowed jumpsuits with the *Vesta Runner*'s insignia and talking loudly about the massive load of fuel cells they were taking to Jupiter and how nervous they were to be traveling through the lawless Cybeles.

If Mox had even one semicompetent spy on Ceres, he would have heard that a juicy prize with a novice crew was heading his way. But what if he were prowling elsewhere or sensed a trap? Tycho wasn't eager to encounter the deadly pirate again, but he also didn't want to think about making a long cruise in the belly of the *Vesta Runner* for nothing.

The communicator chimed.

"*Comet, Ironhawk*, this is Branson," said the clipped voice of the *Vesta Runner's* captain. "We've got a possible sensor contact, fifteen degrees to starboard, forty-five thousand klicks out."

"Acknowledged, *Runner*," Yana said.

She bent over her instruments briefly, then gave up in disgust.

"I can't see anything," Yana said, gesturing out the forward viewports, where nothing was visible except the *Runner's* empty cargo bay. "Probably another false reading, or a rock with slightly-higher-than-expected metal content. By the time that old tub's sensors tell me it's the *Hydra*, I'll be reading the name off her hull."

"Keep your eyes open anyway," Diocletia said. "Remember—"

A massive boom drowned out whatever else she said and left all their ears ringing. The *Comet* lurched sideways, her lights flickering momentarily, and alarms began to blare.

"Impact," Vesuvia reported tonelessly.

"Tycho, maintain communications links," Diocletia said.

"All green," Tycho said, fighting the urge to add "for all the good it's doing us."

"Yana, what's going on out there?" Diocletia asked.

Yana threw up her hands in frustration.

"I don't know!" she yowled. *"Runner, what the heck was that?"*

"Pinnaces!" Branson yelled back. "They're so small, our sensors didn't pick them up! I'm going to open the bay doors—"

"Negative, *Runner*," Diocletia barked. "We're too far out of range. Open up now, and Mox will slip the trap."

"Runner, this is *Ironhawk*," said the voice of Garrett, the other privateer captain. *"Comet*'s right. We'll only get one shot at this. Stand your course."

Tycho gazed at the main screen. A bright cross marked the position of the sensor contact the *Vesta Runner* had made just before she'd been attacked. It was still at least thirty thousand kilometers away. Mox—if that was really him out there—had taken the bait, but he'd been suspicious, using his pinnaces to try to stop the *Runner* well short of his position.

The impact had flung an unwary Huff across the quarterdeck. Now he clanked back to the ladder, magnetic footing engaged, and held on.

"Arrr," he muttered. "Thoadbone always was the tricky one."

The *Comet* jumped again as another blast rattled the *Vesta Runner*. Over the communicator they heard Branson gasp, with voices yelling behind him.

"They're ordering us to heave to!" Branson yelled.

"He's trying to scare you, *Runner*!" Diocletia said. *"Don't you dare stop!"*

"But they'll cut us to pieces!" Branson wailed.

"If you shut down the engines, *I'll* cut you to pieces," Diocletia warned. "Tell them you're having trouble cutting over to manual control—those impacts scrambled the computer interface."

"But—"

"We don't care how you do it," Garrett said. "Just hold them off for three minutes!"

"I'll try," Branson said feebly.

Huff began to chuckle.

"Never send an honest man to do a liar's job," he said.

The *Vesta Runner* continued to creep through space, closing to within 25,000 kilometers of the bright cross on the screen.

"I hate flying blind," Carlo muttered.

"So do I," Diocletia said. "Mr. Grigsby, stand by. I want guns hot and crews ready. And prepare three boarding parties."

"Aye, Captain," Grigsby said. "We're ready—you can count on that."

"Twenty thousand klicks," Yana said.

"Sensor profile complete," Vesuvia said. "Contact is *Hydra*. Confidence ninety-eight point three five percent."

Another explosion rattled the quarterdeck—this one much closer.

"*Ironhawk, Shadow Comet*, this is Branson," the *Runner*'s captain said. He sounded like he could barely breathe. "I told them we had to extinguish the engines manually. I don't think I can get you much closer than five thousand klicks, though—they're already suspicious."

"Captain Branson, listen to me," Diocletia said. "Start slowing at 10,000 klicks and keep your communications channels open so they can hear you. At seven thousand, begin yelling at everybody on your bridge about malfunctions and the computer, and then jam the engines on full ahead."

"They won't believe me—and they'll kill us!" Branson objected.

"Yes, I suspect they will," Diocletia said. "Just like they'll kill you if we lose this fight, or if they find two Jovian privateers in your cargo bay. Too late to turn back now, Captain, so *listen*. Once we come out of that bay, Mox is going to be too busy to worry about you. But you've got to get us close enough. You understand me?"

"I'll do my best," Branson said shakily.

"That will have to do," Diocletia said, closing the channel.

The *Runner* closed to within 20,000 kilometers without attracting more fire from Mox's pinnaces, while the Hashoones grimly watched the distance shrink. At 17,500 kilometers, Huff clattered up the ladderwell to the top deck above, teeth bared in a snarl.

"Ten thousand klicks," Yana said. "Velocity slowing."

"I sure hope Branson understood the plan, Mom," Tycho said.

"Me too," Diocletia muttered.

The *Comet* closed to within 7,000 kilometers. The Hashoones looked at one another, frustrated at not knowing what was happening.

"Why didn't we tell Branson to keep his other channels open to us?" Carlo asked.

"Because I forgot," Diocletia said with a scowl. "Nothing we can do about it now."

Huff clanked back into view, carbines tucked in his belt, a bandolier of stun grenades slung over one shoulder, and a wicked-looking knife clenched in his teeth.

"Not a word out of yeh, yeh cursed electric nanny," he growled around the blade, the words barely understandable through his clenched teeth.

Vesuvia, for once, decided it would be a good idea to stay silent.

"Five thousand," Yana said.

"Come on, Branson!" urged Tycho.

A loud whine began somewhere beneath their feet.

"Velocity increasing," Yana said.

Then another explosion rattled the ship—this one followed by a shriek of torn metal. The *Vesta Runner* shivered and rolled slightly to starboard.

"That was no warning shot," Mavry said. "Mox is playing for keeps now."

"Three thousand!" Yana said.

The *Runner* rumbled, shaking steadily now with impacts.

"Yana, give me a sign at five hundred klicks," Diocletia said. "Captain Branson, Captain Garrett, this is *Comet*. Open the cargo bay when we close to within five hundred klicks. *Ironhawk*, we'll take starboard, you take port."

"We won't last that long!" Branson wailed.

"Two thousand," Yana said.

"Almost there, *Runner*," Garrett said. "Stand your course."

"One thousand," Yana said, raising her voice to be heard over the thud and boom of impacts.

"Carlo, get ready," Diocletia said. "Tycho, monitor all channels. Mr. Grigsby, stand by. Aim for the pinnaces, then the *Hydra*. Yana, eyes and ears peeled. Vesuvia, we'll launch with colors displayed."

"Acknowledged," Vesuvia said.

"Seven fifty!" Yana yelled. They could hear alarms shrieking on the *Runner*'s bridge.

"Here we come, Mox, you chrome-pated buzzard!" Huff roared, transferring the knife from his teeth to his hand.

"Five hundred," Yana said.

"Branson—*GO!*" Diocletia yelled.

They heard the cough and whine of machinery in the bay outside.

"That doesn't sound right," Mavry said.

The cough and whine turned into a clattering rattle.

"The bay doors have been damaged!" Branson yelled. "They're stuck shut!"

15

DEEP SPACE SHOWDOWN

The *Vesta Runner*, her cargo doors jammed shut, took a direct hit and lurched in space. Carlo, Yana, and Tycho exchanged frantic looks.

"Captain Garrett," Diocletia said, "looks like we'll have to blast our way out."

"Agreed," Garrett said grimly.

"Are you both insane?" shrieked Branson.

"Mr. Grigsby, any gun crews that have a clear line of

fire on the cargo bay doors, fire at will," Diocletia said. "Do it now!"

The *Comet*'s guns thundered, the ship shuddering with the continual barrage of fire. The *Vesta Runner*'s cargo bay began to fill with smoke.

"Two hundred klicks," Yana yelled over the roar of the guns.

"Ambient heat in the cargo bay is approaching unsafe levels," Vesuvia said.

"Keep firing, Mr. Grigsby!" Diocletia yelled.

Metal gave way with a shriek, and they saw the blackness of space above the bay. The smoke instantly whisked away into space with the rest of the atmosphere. Belowdecks, the gun crews yelled in triumph.

"Punch it, Carlo!" yelled Diocletia, but her son was already stomping on the throttle and yanking back on the control yoke. The *Shadow Comet* shot upward, out of the *Vesta Runner*'s ruined cargo bay.

Alarms began to scream.

"Proximity warning," Vesuvia said. "Collision imminent."

"Watch out for the *Ironhawk*," Diocletia said.

"Hang on," Carlo warned. He shoved the control yoke and the *Comet* rolled to starboard, away from the *Ironhawk*. Through the viewports, Tycho could see each gun barrel on the other privateer's hull as she cut in front of the *Comet*, maybe ten meters away.

"Whoa," Tycho breathed. "That was close!"

THE JUPITER PIRATES

"Too close," muttered Yana.

Carlo let the *Comet* continue to roll, leaving the Hashoones upside down in their harnesses as the ship turned completely over. Tycho risked a look backward and saw Huff still clamped tightly to the deck, his beard flopped upside down and hiding half his face.

The ship shuddered briefly as her engines scraped the top of the *Vesta Runner*'s hull, and then she was free and right side up once more.

"Mind the paint, son," Mavry said with a smile.

"Vesuvia, damage report," Diocletia said.

"Minimal," Vesuvia said.

The bells rang out—six *clang-clang*s, 0700.

"Mr. Grigsby, fire at will," Diocletia said. "Carlo, full speed and engage the *Hydra*. Yana, find me those pinnaces. And mind your long-range sensors—the Defense Ministry thinks Mox may be working with other pirates."

"Now you tell me?" Yana asked.

"Now I tell you," Diocletia said. "Tycho, scan all channels. If we can't see them coming, maybe we can hear them."

Grigsby's gun crews quickly caught sight of one of the little pirate craft about thirty degrees off the starboard bow. Before the pinnace's startled pilot could react, the *Comet*'s guns turned it into a ball of flame. Cheers came up the ladderwell.

"Good shooting, Mr. Grigsby!" Diocletia said. "Eyes open now—there are still hostiles out there."

"I've got the other pinnace to port, amidships on the

170

Ironhawk," Yana said, hurriedly opening a channel to warn the other privateer's sensor officer. "*Ironhawk*, bandit at two hundred eighty degrees!"

Bolts of energy began lancing out at the *Comet* from a bright dot ahead of them, almost lost in the blackness of space.

"Arr, Thoadbone," growled Huff. "Come out an' play!"

The *Ironhawk*'s crews fired at one of the pinnaces as its guns raked the privateer's hull. Yana's fingers clattered on her keyboard, eyes locked on her scopes.

"Mr. Grigsby," Yana said. "Pinnace at three hundred degrees!"

"We see 'er," Grigsby growled. The *Comet*'s topside turret fired, filling space with brilliant and deadly laser light. The pinnace dodged the burst of fire, rolled back the way it had come—and flew directly into a barrage from the *Ironhawk*.

"We're clear," Diocletia said, staring out the forward port. "Now let's see to Mox."

As if in response, Vesuvia chimed for the crew's attention.

"Incoming transmission from the *Hydra*," she said.

Diocletia smiled.

"Tycho, put it on," she said.

A moment later they were staring at Thoadbone Mox, who was red-faced with fury. His remaining eye widened as he saw the *Comet*'s crew staring back at him.

"Thoadbone Mox," Diocletia said. "You're wanted by the Jovian Union for crimes against its citizenry.

Surrender, and we will take you into custody with no further harm to your crew or your ship. Refuse, and we shall give you no quarter."

"You talk like a policewoman," Mox rasped, peering at the screen. "So, it's the Hashoones. I thought that was yer broken-down antique ship that turned tail and fled two weeks ago. Cursed computer didn't recognize it—must've been all the parts that have fallen off. But *I* knew."

Huff strode forward to stand behind Diocletia. Mox saw him and looked briefly startled. Then he grinned.

"Huff Hashoone," Mox said. "Thought you'd be in a rocking chair by now, sucking dinner through a straw on account of missing half a face."

"Thoadbone Mox," Huff replied. "Thought you'd be space dust by now, on account of missin' half a brain and all of a heart."

Mox cackled. "I've got brain and heart enough to still be captain of my own ship," he said.

Tycho saw Huff's back go rigid with fury. But his grandfather just leaned closer to the screen.

"I ain't captain no more, 'tis true. Know what I am now?" Huff hefted his twin pistols. "Boardin' party. And I'm comin' to settle yer hash."

"Big talk from a half-rusted—" Mox growled.

Diocletia gestured for Tycho to cut the transmission, and the red-faced pirate disappeared in mid rant. The *Hydra* was dead ahead, and Diocletia needed her crew's full attention focused on the enemy ship.

Carlo and the *Ironhawk*'s pilot had spent hours working together in the simulator on their way to the Cybeles, and the effort had paid off. Their positioning was perfect—the *Ironhawk* was perhaps a kilometer to port, about even with the *Comet*.

The two ships passed on either side of the *Hydra*, raking her with broadsides. The dark of space turned blinding white with laser fire. The *Comet* shook continually, jittering and jumping as answering fire from the *Hydra*'s cannons tore into her port side, the impacts flinging the Hashoones around in their harnesses.

"Damage report," Diocletia yelled.

"Third portside gun turret inoperative," Vesuvia reported. "Hull integrity weakened in six points. Atmospheric venting confined by bulkheads."

That was survivable, but if the *Hydra* hit one of those weak points, the damage could be catastrophic. Tycho couldn't help glancing nervously at the patches of pale steel to starboard of the *Comet*'s viewport.

"And the *Hydra*?" Diocletia asked.

"Calculating," Vesuvia said.

"Coming around," Carlo said. He pushed the *Comet* hard to starboard, denying the *Hydra* further shots at her damaged hull armor, then slewed the privateer back the way she'd come, allowing her starboard batteries to open fire on the *Hydra*. On the other side of the pirate ship, the *Ironhawk*'s pilot was matching the *Comet*'s maneuver.

"Make it count, Mr. Grigsby!" Diocletia yelled.

Once again the space around the three ships filled

with fury. Tycho listened to the alarms scream, to the deafening crunches and crashes of laser fire on the hull plates, to the shouts of the gunners belowdecks, to Huff's roars of defiance. Then there was a larger, muffled impact, and the *Comet* streaked past the *Hydra* and came around for a third pass.

As they approached, they saw that the bow of the *Hydra* was cocked upward, as if the ship had been kicked by a giant. Her running lights were dark, her engines unlit.

"Careful—it might be a trick," Diocletia said. "Vesuvia, damage report on the *Hydra*. Yana, watch those long-range sensors. Tycho, ears open."

"Clear for now," Yana said.

"Likewise," Tycho said.

"Calculating," Vesuvia said. "Scans show portside power linkages severed in three places. Confidence ninety-four point six percent."

Huff let out a roar of triumph, and Diocletia and Mavry exchanged brief, satisfied nods. The *Hydra* was dead in space.

"Mr. Grigsby, fire to disarm," Diocletia said. "Boarding parties, prep for action. Carlo, bring us in for docking. Easy now."

As Carlo eased the *Shadow Comet* forward to align her docking ring with that of the *Hydra*, Grigsby's gunners opened fire on the pirate ship's gun turrets, turning her weapons into slag. Tycho realized he was holding his breath, worried that at any second the remaining batteries on Mox's ship would open up and tear into the *Comet* at point-blank range.

"Mavry will lead the first boarding party," Diocletia said. "Carlo, I want you with the second. First boarding party will secure the reactor and engines. Second will take the quarterdeck. Dad will be with the third party, backing up the others as needed. The rest of us will stay here and detach if any other pirates show their faces. Tycho has communications. Yana will run sensors for me."

"I want to be part of a boarding party," Yana said.

"Not now, Yana," Diocletia said.

Carlo tapped the thrusters a final time, and the *Comet*'s docking ring came to rest against that of the *Hydra*, latching tight to it with a clatter of machinery.

"We still have to prove there's a connection between Suud and Mox, and see if we can find our missing Jovians," Diocletia reminded them. "If Mox's crewers can get the power back online, they'll scuttle their computers—and then this was all for nothing."

"Arrr, and remember the *Hydra*'s a prize, Carlo," Huff said. "Don't think the crew of the *Ironhawk* don't know it."

Diocletia nodded. "She is—but we're all Jovians. By all means, get to the quarterdeck first if you can, but nobody shoots anybody over it."

"Got it, Captain," Carlo said, unbuckling his harness and getting to his feet. "We'll make you proud."

Diocletia looked at her oldest son, then at her husband and her father.

"Remember, this isn't a merchant intercept," she said. "The people on the other side of that hatch down there are killers. They aren't expecting quarter, and they won't be giving it."

"As it should be," grunted Huff, sliding down the ladderwell and out of sight. Mavry squeezed his wife's shoulder briefly and followed. Carlo grinned and offered his siblings a jaunty wave, as if he were headed into Port Town for a picnic in a sunny simulation dome. Then he too was gone. Diocletia stared after them for a long moment, then turned to Tycho and Yana, blinking.

"What are your orders?" Tycho asked, but Yana jumped in before Diocletia could answer.

"It's not fair!" she said with a scowl. "Why can't I go?"

"Because if Earth has other pirates out here and we don't see them coming, we're dead," Diocletia said. "Tycho, check your connections with Mavry, Huff, and Carlo. And run the feed through the speakers so we can all hear it."

Tycho nodded.

"Dad, Grandfather—can you hear me?" he asked. "Carlo?"

"It's Dad," Mavry said. "Got you loud and clear."

"I hear yeh, Tyke," rumbled Huff.

"Me too," Carlo said. "We're getting ready to crack open the *Hydra*."

If Carlo was nervous, Tycho couldn't hear it in his voice. His older brother had simulated plenty of hostile boarding actions, as they all had. But no simulation could prepare you for standing in a ring of retainers armed with pistols and knives, knowing that very soon people would be trying to kill you.

"Ranking officer's weapons, First Mate Malone," they heard Grigsby say, and knew he was handing Mavry the traditional chrome musketoons. Tycho had hoped that listening to the familiar ritual would reassure him, but it just made him more anxious.

"Thank you, Mr. Grigsby," Mavry answered solemnly, then raised his voice. "I don't need to tell any of you what's waiting for us. Thoadbone Mox is the kind of Jupiter pirate who gives all of us an evil reputation. He's a murderer and a slaver—and a traitor. Today, he atones for those crimes—crimes against the Jovian Union, his fellow pirates, the families of the missing, and the glory of our good name. Now form up!"

"Three cheers for First Mate Mavry! Three cheers for Captain Huff! Three cheers for Master Carlo!" a crewer yelled, followed by cheers so loud that Tycho had to lift the earpiece away from his head.

"Dobbs! Safrax!" Grigsby yelled. "Point!"

"Captain, boarding parties here," Mavry yelled over the noise. "We're ready."

Diocletia bit her lip, then activated her microphone.

"You are green for boarding," she said. "Godspeed."

Tycho, Yana, and Diocletia heard the clatter of the crewers' weapons, the moan of a hatch opening—and then the staccato sound of blasters firing.

16

BATTLE FOR THE *HYDRA*

Sitting on the quarterdeck of the *Comet*, Tycho, Yana, and Diocletia could only listen to crewers screaming in defiance and pain, the repeated cracks of shots, and the sound of running feet.

"What's happening down there?" Yana demanded of no one in particular.

"Eyes on your scopes," Diocletia reminded her.

Tycho had a layout of a Leopard-class frigate on his screen, with points of light indicating the positions of

Mavry, Carlo, and Huff. All three were wearing tracers on their belts that allowed him to track their progress through Mox's ship.

"One man down," Mavry said into his microphone, breathing hard. "Mox's crewers are resisting, but we're advancing. It's dark—power's completely out."

"I hope the schematics we have for the *Hydra* are accurate," Tycho said to Yana. "If she's been remodeled, they could walk right into a wall—or worse."

Mavry's voice was drowned out as he fired his pistol. Someone screamed.

"The first wave of pirates broke and ran," he said. "We should be at the starboard passageway now. Do you see us, Tycho?"

"Yes," Tycho said, looking at the schematic. "That passageway should run the length of the ship to aft and dead-end at the fire room. Carlo, moving forward you'll hit a T intersection. Turn left, then right, and you should hit the quarterdeck."

"Got it," Carlo said. "I'm heading that way. Mr. Porco and Mr. Richards have lead. It's pitch black. We're feeling our way. Mr. Porco's infrared eye is no use—it's too cold in here."

Tycho tried to imagine feeling his way in the dark aboard a strange ship, not knowing what was waiting for you in the darkness and unable to turn on your headlamp because it would make you an easy target. At least for the moment, being aboard the *Comet* didn't seem so bad.

"Dad, stay where you are," Diocletia said.

THE JUPITER PIRATES

"There's folks on this tub what need holes put in 'em, Dio," Huff objected.

"And Mavry and Carlo may need your help," Diocletia replied. "Sit tight."

Huff grumbled, but the dot of light representing him came to a halt, while Mavry's dot moved slowly toward the *Hydra*'s stern. A moment later Tycho watched as Carlo's dot intersected a wall and kept going.

"Wait, Carlo!" Tycho said.

"What?" his brother demanded.

"Unless you can walk through walls, your schematic's wrong," Tycho said.

"You're right," Carlo said. "Ugh. Everything's different in here."

"They probably reconfigured the layout to make room for the topside gun turrets," Yana said. "Which would mean the ladderwells—"

Suddenly someone yelped and there was a crash, followed by a quick flurry of shouts and curses.

"Porco fell down the ladderwell!" Carlo yelled.

Four shots rang out.

"We've got to help him!" Carlo yelled. "Go! Go! Go!"

They heard Carlo breathing hard, the clatter of feet on ladder rungs—and then a confused mass of shooting and yelling.

"We're belowdecks," Carlo said. "But so is—"

And then he cried out.

Tycho, Yana, and Diocletia leaned forward.

"Carlo! Carlo!" Tycho kept repeating into the microphone.

"Here," Carlo said after a moment. "I—I'm hit, but I think I'll be okay. But we're pinned down! They're all around us!"

"Dad!" Diocletia said. "Carlo—"

"I hear it," Huff said. "C'mon, mateys! Yeh wanna live forever?"

"Still moving aft," Mavry said. "Is Carlo okay?"

Tycho started to answer, but Diocletia cut him off.

"Dad's on it," she said.

For a long moment all they heard was the whistle and whine of shots from Carlo's group and the grunts and tramps of Huff and the Hashoone retainers feeling their way toward his position. Tycho saw Mavry's dot stop and knew his father was wrestling with what to do, desperate to help Carlo but mindful of the mission.

"Continuing aft," Mavry said finally, his dot moving again.

"We're at the ladderwell," Huff said. "Carlo, covering fire. We're comin' down and comin' hard."

"Form up!" Carlo yelled. "Fire all directions!"

Tycho heard a clang and a clatter that had to be his grandfather's metal feet hitting the decking at the foot of the ladderwell, and saw the dots representing him and Carlo converge. Then they heard firing and yelling, broken by Huff's roars and some impressively awful oaths. Huff yelled in pain, then opened fire with his forearm cannon, cursing steadily.

"How d'ye like that for payback, you slaver rat?" Huff growled, his voice strained. "I've got Carlo. But it's hard fightin' down here, Captain."

"Are you all right?" Diocletia asked.

"Flesh wound from a lucky shot," Huff muttered. "But we'll be a while flushing this lot out of their holes. Someone needs to secure the quarterdeck."

Tycho looked at the dots—Huff and Carlo together, Mavry aft.

"We can double back—" Mavry began, then cursed as blaster fire began bursting around him, too.

"Stick to the plan," Diocletia said. She stood and began gathering things from beneath her station.

"I'll go, Captain," Yana said.

"No, I need you on the scans," Diocletia said. "And to fly the *Comet* if more pirates arrive. Tycho—"

"If there are still pirates out there, you should fly the ship, Mom," Tycho said. "You don't need a navigator, but you do need Yana to run scans—she's the best at it. *I'm* the one who should go. As long as Yana can handle communications."

"I can handle anything on this ship," Yana said. "Except pistols, apparently."

"That's enough, Yana," Diocletia warned.

She looked at her son for a long moment, frowning, and Tycho could see the doubt on her face.

"I'm ready for this, Captain," he said, hoping that was true.

Diocletia shut her eyes for a moment. Then she opened them and nodded.

"Go," she said. "I'll order another boarding party put together from the portside gun crews. I just wish we had more able spacers. Stay behind the retainers, Tycho. Get to the quarterdeck and hold it."

Tycho leaped to his feet, passing his headset over to Yana. He reached under his workstation, thinking, *It's just like the simulator. Vest. Gloves. Tracer. Headlamp. Pistol. One step at a time.*

He zipped his vest and ran through the checklist one last time, then nodded at his mother and sister.

"Ready, Captain," he said.

"Good luck," Diocletia said. Then her gaze softened and she was staring at him, no longer the captain but his mother.

"Be careful, Tyke," she said.

Belowdecks, it smelled like sweat, smoke, and burned circuitry. Seven Hashoone retainers were waiting for Tycho at the airlock, carbines in their hands. They saw him and snapped to attention.

Tycho looked at them, momentarily surprised. Most of them were just a few years older than he was, and they looked wild-eyed and scared. He supposed he shouldn't have been shocked—the *Comet*'s most reliable retainers had all been assigned to the earlier boarding parties, and this was what was left.

It would have to do, Tycho thought.

"I'll make this fast," Tycho said as he checked his carbine's power levels. "Our target is the quarterdeck. We're to secure her computers—and if we can, take her as a prize. Let's go."

"Three cheers for Master Tycho!" said Croke, a retainer with a white beard and a mouth full of black ceramic teeth. He'd been the *Comet*'s purser once, in charge of her finances, till his fondness for drink had landed him on the blacklist one too many times. Tycho sure hoped that wasn't a problem now.

"It's an honor to fight alongside you, gentlemen," Tycho said, stepping behind Croke and two very young retainers—Higgs and Tully were their names, he remembered. Two more men, Laney and Chin, stepped behind him to protect their rear, leaving two retainers behind to guard the airlock.

"Yana, can you hear me?" Tycho asked.

"Loud and clear."

"Good. I'm shutting down the others' channels—it's too easy to get lost or distracted in there."

"I'll tell you anything you need to hear," Yana said.

"I know you will," Tycho said. "We're ready, *Comet*."

"You are green for boarding," Diocletia said.

Tycho gave the order, and the retainers rushed through the short passage connecting the two ships and leading into the gloom beyond. The *Hydra* smelled bad, like stale air and roasted meat, and Tycho could hear blaster fire. The men leading Tycho's group switched on their headlamps just long enough to illuminate the passageway.

"That's enough—shut them off," Tycho said. "If there are any Hydras left, we'll be easy targets."

Higgs reached up and fumbled with his lamp. His hand was shaking.

The lamps went off, plunging them into darkness. Tycho crept along behind the men, peering at the dimly lit schematic strapped to his forearm. Someone cursed, and a moment later Tycho stumbled over something. Laney turned on his light, and Tycho was staring at a dead pirate, mouth open in a terrible surprised O. He stepped gingerly over the man's body.

"It's an unlucky sight, boys, but don't let it rattle yeh," Croke whispered. "That one had it comin', signin' on with a traitor like Mox."

Tycho nodded and Laney shut off the light, leaving them in darkness again. They picked their way forward, occasionally stepping over other bodies lying twisted on the deck with unseeing eyes.

Suddenly Tycho felt unsteady on his feet, then found himself floating. One of the retainers cried out.

"Steady," Tycho told them. "Activate the magnets in your gloves and boots. We can work our way along the walls. *Comet*, we're fine, but we've lost artificial gravity."

"Auxiliary generator probably ran out of charge," Yana said in his ear.

The firing ahead of them had stopped. Tycho looked at his schematic and realized this was where Carlo's group had gotten lost. He turned on his lamp and saw they were in a narrow room with two ladderwells instead of the maze of passageways shown on the schematic. Pistols and a knife were spinning slowly through the air.

Tycho signaled to the retainers, and they kicked with their hands and feet until they reached the wall, where they locked onto the metal, the magnets in their gloves clicking faintly. They shut off the lamps and began to work their way around the perimeter of the room in the darkness, lifting their hands and feet one at a time and clanking along the wall.

As they worked, Tycho told Yana what he'd seen of the room's layout.

"I think I know what modifications they made," Yana said. "In about five meters you should reach a short passageway leading to the quarterdeck."

"Tycho, *Ironhawk*'s boarding party has entered the *Hydra*," Diocletia said.

"Does that mean 'Careful not to shoot them' or 'Get to the quarterdeck before they do'?" asked Tycho.

"Both," his mother said.

They reached the spot Yana had told them to aim for, but instead of the emptiness of a passageway, their fingers found the outline of a sealed door. Tycho and four retainers—Higgs, Tully, Croke, and Laney—turned on their lamps and took up positions on either side of the door, with the last retainer, Chin, clinging to the ceiling like a spider. They shut off the lights, and Tycho thumbed the door control. Nothing happened.

"Break it down, Mr. Croke," he said.

"Tycho!" Yana said urgently in his ear. "Dad says

another gang of Hydras got behind them—they're headed your way!"

Tycho spun, lifting his gloves off the walls too quickly. His upper body began to float, and he hurriedly felt for the wall again. He pulled out his earpiece and could hear yelling. The voices were getting closer.

"Enemy coming at us!" Tycho yelled. "Look to your rear! Tully, shut off that cursed light!"

A laser bolt struck high on the wall near Chin, dazzling Tycho's eyes. He heard the thump of the Hydras kicking off the walls of the passageway to hurl themselves through the air in zero gravity, screaming as they came. Another laser blast gouged the decking below Tycho's feet.

Just like the simulator, Tycho reminded himself, trying to force himself to breathe. But of course it wasn't anything like the simulator. Wounds here were real, and those who died stayed dead.

"There's too many—they'll gun us down!" Higgs screamed, firing his carbine at the oncoming pirates. His eyes were huge and wild. In the sudden light from the shots, Tycho saw Chin windmilling his arms, trying to reestablish contact with the wall. Tully was fumbling for his blaster.

"Higgs! Chin! Tully!" Tycho yelled. "Stand your ground! STAND YOUR GROUND! You are Comets, men, and you will defend crew and country!"

Tycho drew his pistol, reaching behind him to press the magnets in the glove on his free hand against the wall. *Short, controlled bursts,* he thought.

Then the pirates were among them, screaming and firing. Flashes of laser fire lit up the darkness, giving Tycho crazy, jumbled glimpses of Comets and pirates firing, yelling, tumbling away from the walls. Carbines cracked and thudded, and a spear of laser light zipped by Tycho's ear, close enough to scorch his skin and fill his nostrils with the smell of burning hair. Someone smashed into him, sending him spinning in the zero gravity, and he fumbled for the wall, his pistol jerking in his hand as he fired again and again, screaming at the top of his lungs.

Then Croke was gripping his shoulder, mouth close to his ear.

"Easy, Master Hashoone," he said soothingly. "It's done."

Croke had turned his headlamp on. Five of Mox's pirates were still and silent, floating through the air. So was Chin, hand clutched to his throat, eyes empty. Higgs was hugging his arm to his side, teeth bared in a grimace.

"Tyke!" Yana was yelling in his ear. "What's happening?"

"We lost Chin, but the rest of us are all right," Tycho said, gasping for breath.

"Acknowledged," Diocletia said. "You need to keep moving."

Tycho shut his eyes for a moment, trying to force his hands to stop shaking.

"Aye-aye," he said. "Proceeding to the quarterdeck. Mr. Croke, I need this door open."

"You'll want to back up a bit, Master Hashoone," Croke said. "Laney, bit of light, if you please?"

Tycho crept backward a couple of steps and shielded his eyes as Croke set his carbine on continuous fire and began to burn through the lock, which was soon glowing cherry red. Tycho tried not to gag at the stench of burning wiring.

"Tully, lend a hand 'ere," Croke grunted. "You lot cover us."

Securing themselves on the wall, Croke and Tully kicked at the melted lock. It groaned, and the door rattled open.

"Go!" barked Croke, and the men pushed forward into the narrow passageway beyond the door, carbines raised. Tycho kicked off the wall and followed them.

The *Hydra*'s quarterdeck was dimly lit by starlight. Croke, pistol in each hand, guarded a trio of Mox's crewers, who had their arms raised. Tully and Laney were behind him, braced against the back wall of the quarterdeck.

"The quarterdeck is yours, Master Hashoone," Croke said with a grin.

Just then another door slid open on the other side of the room, and five men surged through the gap, swimming through the air with pistols raised. Croke, Tully, and Laney whirled, aiming their weapons at the new arrivals.

"No!" Tycho yelled. "They're Ironhawks!"

The men from the *Ironhawk* and the *Comet* stared at

one another, fingers perilously close to their triggers. Tycho locked eyes with the leader, who had a black beard. The man's eyes moved to the captain's chair.

Tycho kicked himself off the back wall as hard as he could, aware that the lead crewer from the *Ironhawk* had done the same. He overshot the captain's chair but caught it with his foot, swinging himself around and grabbing the back with both hands.

"Tycho Hashoone, bridge crew of the *Shadow Comet*," he said, the words tumbling out so fast that they were more noise than speech.

The other man bashed his knee into Mox's workstation and grunted, floating across the quarterdeck.

Suddenly the artificial gravity returned, slamming Tycho and everyone else to the deck. Tycho landed flat on his back, the impact driving the air out of his lungs. The two boarding parties sprang to their feet with groans and curses, then aimed their guns at one another again.

"Gravity's back on," Yana reported.

"You don't say," Tycho muttered, still a bit shaky. He got to his feet and saw the *Ironhawk*'s mate still picking himself off the deck. Before the other man could move, Tycho put his hand back on Mox's chair.

"According to the laws of war and having achieved victory through course of arms, I claim this craft on behalf of the Jovian Union," Tycho said. "She and her contents will be apportioned according to the laws of space as adjudicated by the Ceres Admiralty Court."

The *Ironhawk*'s mate hesitated. Croke moved his

carbine uncertainly between the prisoners and the other privateers. Then the *Ironhawk's* mate shook his head in disgust, holstering his pistol.

"Stand down, men," he said. "She's yours, kid."

17

SECRETS IN
THE CYBELES

An hour later, the power was back on and the bodies of sixteen of Mox's pirates had been removed from the *Hydra*'s decks, along with those of five Hashoone retainers and two crewers from the *Ironhawk*. On the *Hydra*'s quarterdeck, Diocletia and Captain Garrett of the *Ironhawk* stood with Tycho, watching as Mavry and Yana tried to break into the *Hydra*'s logs.

"I congratulate you on your prize, Master Hashoone," said Garrett, a handsome man with red hair and dark eyes.

"First Mate McRae wasn't happy about it but said your acrobatics were quite the thing to see. Can't say I've ever claimed a bridge in zero gravity myself. What's it like?"

"Kind of fun, except for the landing," Tycho said.

Garrett smiled and nodded.

"Any luck?" Diocletia asked Mavry and Yana.

Mavry shook his head. Mox's bridge crew had locked down the files, and so far no threat had proved frightening enough to persuade them to unlock them.

"They're more scared of Mox than they are of anyone else," Diocletia said with a sigh.

"Shame that Mox escaped," Garrett said.

"We saw the gig launch, at the end of the fighting," Yana said. "But we didn't have the right angle to take a shot at it."

"We had the angle, but it didn't matter," Garrett said, shaking his head. "It was out of range before our gunners could punch through its armor."

The rest of the news was good, though. Mavry had discovered eighteen Jovians locked in the *Hydra*'s hold, the crew of a freighter intercepted by the *Hydra* three days before. With the Jovians freed, the hold now served as a brig for Mox's pirates. Carlo and Huff were back there now, looking for the man from Yana's photo. And Tycho was going through security camera footage, trying to spot anything Mox's pirates might have hidden during the battle.

They all turned at the sound of footsteps. Huff, Carlo, and Grigsby entered the quarterdeck, the man from the photo walking dejectedly between them. The *Comet's* surgeon had bandaged Carlo's face and given Huff a sling for his flesh-and-blood arm.

"It's nothing, Mother," Carlo said, noticing Diocletia's eyes on him. "Blaster shot grazed my cheek."

"The lad will heal," Huff said. "An' have a scar to make the girlies in port go wild."

"What about you, Dad?" Diocletia asked.

"Bit more than a graze," Huff admitted, pulling back the sling. Tycho gasped. His grandfather's right hand was gone, vaporized in combat.

"Now don't go cryin' over me," Huff growled. "Bit less flesh and a bit more metal is all. That hand did nothin' but pain me anyhow."

"Speaking of which, your indicators are starting to flash red," Diocletia said. "Why don't you go back to the *Comet* to recharge?"

"Arrr," Huff muttered, glancing at the readouts in his chest. "Too much excitement."

As the *Hydra's* bells rang out four times, Huff stomped off and Diocletia turned to Carlo and the sour-faced man from the photo. Yana came to stand by her mother's side.

"Like I already told them, I'm not giving you any passwords," he said.

"Mm-hmm," said Diocletia. "What's your name, crewer?"

"Joss Roke," the man said.

"Well, Joss Roke," Diocletia said. "You've been found working for a known pirate, murderer, and slaver, with a hold full of Jovian citizens whose craft was illegally intercepted."

"I'm just bridge crew," Roke objected. "Signed on at Ceres. I never heard of Thoadbone Mox before—thought he was a legal privateer. Once we were out here and I saw things were different, what could I do?"

Diocletia smiled at the man.

"I *am* a legal privateer, Mr. Roke," she said. "So I'm acquainted with the penalties for the crimes Mox has committed. Do you know what they are, Mr. Roke?" Diocletia took a step closer to Roke, her voice quiet. "You'll *hang*, Mr. Roke," she said. "It's a bad way to die. What *might* keep you alive is to tell us everything."

Roke swallowed but shook his head.

"You want me to turn on Thoadbone Mox?" he asked. "You must be crazy, lady."

Grigsby cocked his carbine and stuck it under Roke's chin, eyes blazing.

"Respect," he said in a cold voice.

"Go ahead," Roke said. "Mox will do a lot worse."

"Mr. Grigsby, that's not necessary," Diocletia said. She nodded at Yana, who showed Roke her mediapad and the photograph of him standing next to Suud's aide and Hindman.

Roke went pale. Yana grinned.

"Nobody's asking you to turn on Thoadbone Mox," Diocletia said. "We're asking you to turn on Threece Suud."

* * *

After a bit more convincing, Joss Roke gave up the password for the *Hydra*'s computer system—to Huff's amusement, it was the name of Mox's grandmother. Once they had the password, Tycho sped through views recorded by the *Hydra*'s internal and external cameras, while Yana inspected the transmissions Mox's ship had sent and received. Meanwhile, Mavry and Carlo began searching through the logs. They were full of evidence—meticulous records about everything from ships intercepted to ports visited.

The Hashoones recognized seven names as being among the sixteen Jovian craft that had gone missing. And Mavry quickly noticed something odd: after every intercept, the *Hydra* had climbed high above the plane of the solar system, visiting a slightly different point each time.

"How do you explain that?" Mavry asked his children.

"Easy," Carlo said, pressing a cold pack onto his cheek. "It's an asteroid in an irregular orbit. Nobody who didn't already know it existed would ever find it."

"Which makes it the perfect pirate hideout," Tycho said.

"But despite what the Defense Ministry said, the logs don't show Mox working with any other pirates," Mavry said. "And he went there only after intercepting Jovian craft."

"So you're saying it isn't a pirate hideout?" Tycho asked. "Then what is it?"

"Let's find out," Mavry said. "I have my suspicions, though."

Tycho had something he had to do first. While the rest of the Hashoones were busy, he slipped back to the *Comet*. Huff was in his cramped cabin, plugged into the power unit that recharged his cybernetic parts.

"Tyke," Huff said, delighted to be visited. "You did well back there, lad."

"Grandfather, I was looking at the internal security cameras," Tycho said.

"Mox had security cameras?" Huff asked. "Huh. Didn't peg ol' Thoadbone as so conscientious."

"I saw what you did," Tycho said.

"So are you going to report me?" Huff asked. "They'll put me in prison, yeh know. That or worse."

Tycho considered.

"No," he said. "I'm not going to report you. But you have to tell Mom. And the others."

"Okay, Tycho," Huff said. "When things are settled, I will. Captain's honor."

Tycho nodded and turned to go. But then he stopped at the cabin door and looked back.

"Can you tell me why you did it?" he asked his grandfather.

"When I tell the rest, I'll tell yeh that too," Huff said.

Tycho nodded and returned to the corridor. He put his foot on the first rung of the ladderwell, then heard the sound of drawers opening nearby. Stepping away from the ladderwell, he poked his head into the cuddy and found that Diocletia had returned from the *Hydra* and was brewing a cup of coffee.

"Tycho," she said. "You did very well back there. I'm proud of you."

Tycho ducked his head, then smiled.

"I was just happy to do something useful," he said.

"What do you mean by that?" Diocletia asked, sipping her coffee.

Tycho hesitated, but it was too late.

"Let's face it," he said. "Running communications and plotting navigation are the two least important jobs on the ship."

He scowled, wishing he hadn't said anything, that he hadn't followed up his good work aboard the *Hydra* with a complaint that would earn him a rebuke and get recorded in the Log.

Diocletia put down her coffee cup and crossed the cuddy to stand in front of him. She took his face in her hands so that he had to look up at her.

"Tycho, listen to me," she said with a smile. "Talking to people and knowing where to go are the most important jobs a captain has."

The *Vesta Runner*'s cargo bay doors were beyond repair, but the bay itself hadn't been damaged when the *Shadow Comet* and the *Ironhawk* blasted their way free. That allowed the two privateers to settle back into their cradles for the long trip to the mysterious asteroid above the solar system. Leading the freighter on the voyage was the *Hydra*, hastily repaired and attached to her long-range tanks. She was now piloted by Carlo, with Yana and Tycho filling out his temporary bridge crew.

"Would you look at that?" Yana said wonderingly as they neared the asteroid. It was long and flat, perhaps a kilometer long, and tumbling in an eccentric orbit through deep space, so far from the regular spacelanes that it made the Cybeles seem well traveled.

But it wasn't lifeless. Yana put the results of her scan on the *Hydra*'s main screen. The surface of the asteroid was dotted with pressure domes and pitted with mines.

"That's a huge operation," Tycho said with a long whistle.

"Yep," Carlo said. "A corporate factory of that size must demand a lot of labor. And I think we can all guess where they've been getting some of their workers. You were right, Tyke. It is a slave camp."

"I didn't say anything," Tycho said, but he couldn't resist grinning at Carlo.

"Incoming transmission," grumbled the *Hydra*'s artificial intelligence, a rather disagreeable program that responded—sometimes—to the name Atticus.

"Put it through, Atticus," said Tycho. "No visuals on our side of the transmission."

The main screen flickered, and the Hashoones were confronted by a scruffy, irate-looking man in a stained jumpsuit.

"Mox!" he yelled. "You're late! We have shipments ready for transit back to GlobalRex! And did you bring me new laborers?"

"*Comet* and *Ironhawk* are launching from the *Vesta*

Runner," Yana reported.

"You can turn the video feed on now, Atticus," Tycho said.

The man stopped complaining and stared at his screen, clearly confused.

"I beg your pardon," Carlo said. "There was a slight delay while we were capturing Mox's ship. Oh, and you might want to prepare for a visit, sir. Starships from the news media and the Jovian Defense Force are about a day behind us, and they're really interested in what you and GlobalRex have been up to out here."

18

CASE CLOSED

hreece Suud sat glumly in his chair in the Ceres
Admiralty Court, in a plain black suit. Around him,
the courtroom was filled to bursting with unhappy-
looking bureaucrats from Earth, dour GlobalRex corporate mandarins, smiling Jovian officials, boisterous *Comet*
crewers, Hashoone retainers, and members of the news
media, all of them jostling and quarreling.

"All rise for the Honorable Uribel Quence," said the
bailiff.

Judge Quence was looking his best. He was wearing a new, freshly powdered wig, for once resting in the proper position atop his head, and his droopy cheeks had been slathered in makeup to ensure he wouldn't look shiny in the news video feeds. Even the fake plants had been given a good dusting.

"Be seated," Judge Quence said. He gave Diocletia and Tycho a brief nod where they sat at their table, then turned to Suud.

"Secretary Suud," Judge Quence said. "I understand you have a statement you'd like to make?"

"Indeed I do, Your Honor," Suud said, getting to his feet and scanning the rows of camera operators. "Though the recent, um, *newsworthy* events in the outer solar system do not directly concern this court, I would like to say a few words about them. Let me express both to Your Honor and to all those watching how shocked and appalled I am to discover that a low-ranking member of my staff was engaged in illegal activities connected with a notorious pirate such as Thoadbone Mox."

Suud paused for a moment to look into the cameras and bite his lip.

"As for the scurrilous allegations that I, as a representative of the Earth government, knew of such activities, they are irresponsible and completely untrue," Suud continued. "If I'd had the slightest suspicion that a member of my staff was violating the law, I can assure you I myself would have marched him to the nearest law enforcement office. I have spent the last several days in close consultation with the authorities on Earth and with GlobalRex's internal review board, and we intend to conduct a thorough investigation with full cooperation from all branches of the company, its subsidiaries, and His Majesty's government."

Suud nodded at the judge and bowed his head.

"Thank you, Secretary," Judge Quence said. "I'm glad to hear you'll have help, because you're going to be busy. Earlier proceedings in this case concerned the legal definition of a diplomat. That question must be settled by Earth and the Jovian Union. But this court will not sit idle while diplomatic credentials are issued to employees of enterprises involved in a criminal conspiracy. Therefore, effective immediately, no diplomatic credentials issued by Earth within the last year will be recognized by any admiralty court. What's more, this court rules that the Hashoone family is entitled to the cargo captured from the *Cephalax II*, full ransoms of crew and craft, and the *Hydra* as a prize of war."

The Comets leaped to their feet, whooping and laughing. Judge Quence gaveled them into silence with considerable difficulty, then jabbed one thick finger at Suud.

"Let this be a lesson to you or your successor, Secretary Suud, and to your masters on Earth and at GlobalRex," he said. "My court will not be used for cheap stunts or dirty dealing. Adjourned."

Judge Quence banged his gavel on the podium and vanished into his chambers. As the courtroom once again dissolved into a tumult, Diocletia elbowed Tycho and inclined her chin across the room. Suud was pushing his way toward them, the corners of his mouth turned down. Standing up behind his wife and son, Mavry put his hand on Tycho's shoulder.

"Can we help you, Secretary?" Tycho asked when Suud got close enough.

"You can help me, Master Hashoone, by reconsidering the dangerous and illegal career you have chosen for yourself," snapped Suud, his cheeks red. "You may be celebrating today, but beware tomorrow. That goes for your brother and sister, too. You're all on a road to ruin."

He stalked off and was swallowed up by a horde of baying journalists. Mavry watched him go, then smiled.

"What a nice man," he said. "It's rare to find a citizen of Earth who's so concerned with the welfare of Jovian children."

The Jovian officials stationed on Ceres waited until after the afternoon's brief celebration to pull Diocletia aside and tell her that the Hashoones wouldn't get to keep the *Hydra* despite Judge Quence's ruling—Mox's ship had been seized as part of a criminal investigation into the asteroid factory where the captive Jovians had toiled as slaves for GlobalRex.

Tycho, Yana, and Carlo were outraged, but Diocletia just shrugged.

"Oh, I knew they'd do it," she said. "Carina's already filed the documents to fight for possession in admiralty court. But it's not all bad—the *Ceph Two* is our prize, and the Union gave us head money for recovering its citizens safe and sound. Not bad for a few weeks' work."

Tycho smiled, but his mother wasn't finished.

"All three of you kids did a remarkable job," Diocletia said. "Yana, none of this good fortune would have happened if you hadn't paid attention in port and insisted that leads be followed, even when none of us believed you. Carlo, if you hadn't performed some remarkable maneuvers, we'd be dead or hoping someone might come and rescue *us*. And Tycho, you not only fought bravely aboard the *Hydra* but were the one who saw patterns beneath apparent chaos . . . connections no one else saw. Threece Suud is a smart adversary, but you were smarter—and the entire Jovian Union ought to be grateful."

Tycho mumbled his thanks.

"But let me tell you all what makes me most proud," Diocletia said. "It's that when it mattered, you three stopped your quarreling and worked admirably as a team. It's true that only one of you can be captain of the *Shadow Comet*, but any ship in the Jovian Union would be lucky to have you in her crew."

Carlo grinned, his new scar crinkling his cheek. Yana nodded. Tycho leaned back, deciding just to enjoy the moment.

"I don't agree with the Union taking the *Hydra* from us, seeing how we won that prize fair and square," Mavry said. "Funny thing, though—I made a mistake searching through her computers, looking for information about those nine other Jovian ships. I'm afraid I accidentally downloaded her logs to the *Comet*'s memory. You'd be surprised how many intriguing chemical signatures and sightings Vesuvia's already found in there."

Tycho looked at his father, astonished, while Carlo shook his head in amusement and Yana threw back her head and laughed. Huff looked up from the new metal hand he'd had fashioned out of gleaming chrome.

"You broke ol' Mox's ciphers?" he asked, surprised.

"Some of them," Mavry said. "There's a lot still locked away, but with enough time we'll crack those too."

Tycho caught his grandfather's eye, and Huff nodded.

"I've got summat to say meself," Huff grunted.

"What's that, Dad?" Diocletia asked, smiling.

"I let Mox go."

The smile faded from Diocletia's face. The Hashoones were silent for a moment.

"You did what?" Carlo burst out.

"I let him take the *Hydra*'s gig," Huff said. "An' I ain't sorry, neither."

Diocletia gaped at him.

"Why would you do such a thing?" she asked. "Thoadbone Mox is a traitor—a slaver and worse."

"Aye, but he's summat better, too," Huff said, his chin held high. *"He's a pirate."*

"What do you mean, Grandfather?" asked Yana.

"Everything we been through, it's a game played by politicians, and we're the pawns," Huff said, scratching his bearded chin with the stub of his blaster. "In a few more years, Dio, this'll be your solar system, and all us real pirates will be out of the way. But we ain't gone quite yet."

"You're nothing like Thoadbone Mox, Grandfather," Tycho objected.

"Yeh might be surprised, laddie," Huff said. "Mox an' me understand each other. If I ever see him again, I'll try an' blow a hole in him—but I'll not help put him in a cell. Let him die among the stars, like all us old pirates deserve."

A SPACER'S LEXICON

A

abaft. To the rear of.

able spacer. The most experienced class of crewer aboard a starship. Able spacers are more experienced than ordinary spacers, while crewers with too little experience to be considered ordinary spacers are called "dirtsiders."

admiralty court. A court concerned with the laws of space, including the taking of prizes. The Jovian Union maintains several admiralty courts in the Jupiter system and abides by the decisions of the admiralty court on the neutral minor planet Ceres, with privateers and warships expected to report to the admiralty court with jurisdiction over the area of space where a prize is taken.

aft. Toward the rear of a starship; the opposite of fore.

air scrubber. A collection of filters and pumps that remove carbon dioxide and impurities from the air aboard a starship, keeping it healthy and (relatively) clean.

amidships. In the middle of a starship.

armorer. A crewer in charge of a starship's hand weapons. Most crewers on privateers and pirate ships carry their own arms.

arrrr. Originally an acknowledgment of an order ("yar"), it has become a nonspecific pirate outburst, adaptable to any situation. The more Rs, the greater the intensity of feeling.

articles. A written agreement drawn up for each cruise, setting out rules and the division of any prize money and signed by all hands aboard a privateer or pirate ship.

articles of war. The body of space law governing hostilities between spacegoing nations and their starships.

avast. Stop!

aviso. A small, speedy starship used for carrying messages across space.

aye-aye. An acknowledgment of an order.

B

bandit. An enemy starship, typically a small,

maneuverable one that's likely to attack you.

bandolier. A belt slung over an arm or across the chest that holds carbines, ammunition pouches, and other nasty things.

barky. An affectionate nickname for one's own starship.

beam. The side of a ship, always identified as port or starboard.

beat to quarters. A summons to battle stations, in ancient times accomplished by beating out a rhythm on a drum, in modern times achieved by playing a recording.

belay. A ranking officer's order countermanding a just-issued order.

belowdecks. The deck of a starship below the bridge or quarterdeck, generally reserved for spacers and officers who aren't members of the bridge crew. "Belowdecks" also refers collectively to these spacers.

berth. A sleeping place aboard a starship.

bilge. In ancient seagoing ships, the lowest part of a hull, which filled with foul water also called bilge. In modern parlance, anything foul or nonsensical.

blacklist. A list of spacers to be punished for failure to properly perform their duties or for other breaches of discipline.

blackstrap. Cheap, sweet wine bought in ports.

black transponder. A transponder that identifies a starship as belonging to a pirate captain, or more commonly transmits a blank identification.

blaster. A pistol or other handheld carbine.

boarding action. The invasion of a starship with marines or crewers.

boarding party. A group of marines or crewers whose job it is to board and take control of a starship.

bogey. A starship that has been seen on scopes but not yet identified.

bosun. A crewer whose duties include daily ship inspections. The bosun reports to the warrant officer.

bow. The front of a starship.

bow chaser. A gun located at a starship's bow, designed for firing at ships being pursued.

bridge. A starship's command center, generally called the quarterdeck on warships, privateers, and pirate ships. On the *Shadow Comet*, the quarterdeck is the middle deck and reserved for the bridge crew.

bridge crew. The officers who serve aboard the quarterdeck or bridge. On many privateers, the bridge crew is limited to the family that owns the ship or its close associates.

bridle port. A port in a ship's bow through which the bow chasers extend.

brig. A room used as a jail aboard a starship.

broadside. A volley of shots aimed at the side of an enemy ship, delivered at close range.

bulk freighter. A large merchant ship, typically corporate owned.

bulkhead. A vertical partition dividing parts of a starship. In the event of a breach, bulkheads seal to isolate damage and prevent the atmosphere from escaping.

buoy. A marker defining a spacelane. In the modern age, buoys send electronic signals to starships and maintain position through small, efficient engines.

burdened vessel. A starship that doesn't have the right-of-way; not the privileged vessel.

burgoo. A gruel made from shipboard rations, not particularly liked by crewers.

C

cabin. An enclosed room on a starship. Generally refers to an officer's personal quarters.

cannon. A general term for a starship's hull-mounted weapons. Cannons can fire laser beams or missiles and are designed for various intensities of fire and ranges.

captain. The commander of a starship. Traditionally, a former captain is still addressed as "Captain."

carbine. A pistol.

cargo. Goods carried by a merchant starship.

cargo hauler. A no-frills class of freighter, typically corporate owned.

carronade. A powerful, short-range projectile cannon used in combat.

cartel ship. A starship transporting prisoners to an agreed-upon port. Cartel ships are exempt from capture or recapture while on their voyages, provided they don't engage in commerce or warlike acts.

cashier. To discharge a crewer.

caulk. Thick rubber used to plug holes and seams in a starship's hull.

chamade. A signal requesting a cessation of hostilities and negotiations.

chandler. A merchant who sells goods to starships in port.

cheroot. A cheap, often smelly cigar.

chronometer. A timepiece.

coaster. A starship that operates close to a planet or within a system of moons, as opposed to starships that make interplanetary voyages.

cold pack. A flexible packet kept cold and used to numb minor injuries.

condemn. To seize a ship for auction or sale under prize law.

container ship. A large merchant ship that typically carries cheap bulk goods.

convoy. A group of merchant ships traveling together for mutual protection, often with armed starships as escorts.

corvette. A small, fast, lightly armed warship.

crewer. A member of a starship's crew; the equivalent of sailors on ancient ships. "Crewer" technically refers to all members of a starship's crew, but members of the bridge crew are rarely if ever called crewers.

crimp. A person who captures spacers in port and sells them to starships as crewers, usually by working with a press gang. Navy officers who lead authorized press gangs are never called crimps—at least, not to their faces.

crowdy. A thick porridge. More edible than burgoo, but not by much.

cruise. A starship's voyage.

cruiser. A fast, heavily armed warship.

cuddy. A cabin in which officers gather to eat their meals.

cutter. A scout ship.

D

dead lights. Eyes.

derelict. Cargo left behind after a shipwreck with no expectation of recovery. Any claimant may legally salvage derelict.

destroyer. A small warship with the speed to hunt down small, nimble attackers.

dirtside. A spacer's term for being off one's ship on a planet or moon. Said with faint derision and distress.

dirtsider. A spacer with minimal training and experience, limited to simple tasks aboard a starship. A hardworking dirtsider may eventually be rated an ordinary spacer.

dog watch. Either of the two short watches between 1600 and 2000. At two hours, a dog watch is half the duration of a normal watch.

dreadnought. A large, well-armed but slow warship.

dromond. A very large merchant ship, often one that carries expensive goods.

dry dock. A facility where starships are taken out of

service for substantial repairs or refitting.

duff. A kind of pudding served as a treat aboard starships.

E

engineer. The crewer or officer responsible for keeping a starship operating properly.

engine room. The control room for a starship's engines. Sometimes the same as the fire room.

ensign. A flag indicating a starship's allegiance.

escort. A starship providing protection for another vessel, typically one that is unarmed.

F

fanlight. A portal over the door of an officer's cabin, providing light and air while maintaining privacy.

fenders. Bumpers on the sides of a starship, used to protect against damage in crowded shipyards, on landing fields, or in parking orbits.

fire room. The control room for a starship's reactor.

Sometimes the same as the engine room.

fireship. A starship loaded with munitions and exploded among enemy ships to damage them.

first mate. A starship's second-in-command.

flagship. The starship commanded by the ranking officer in a task force or fleet.

flip. A strong beer favored by crewers.

flotsam. Debris and objects left floating in space after a starship is damaged or destroyed.

flummery. A shipboard dessert.

fore. Toward the front of a starship; the opposite of aft.

forefoot. The foremost part of a starship's lower hull.

freighter. A general term for a merchant vessel.

frigate. A fast warship used for scouting and intercepts, well armed but relying more on speed than weapons. The *Shadow Comet,* the *Ironhawk,* and the *Hydra* are heavily modified frigates.

G

galleon. A large merchant ship, particularly one that carries expensive cargoes.

galley. The kitchen on a starship.

gangway. The ramp leading into a ship, lowered when a ship is on a landing field.

gibbet. A post with a protruding arm from which criminals sentenced to death are hanged.

gig. A small, unarmed ship used for short trips between nearby moons or between ports and starships in orbit. An armed gig is generally called a launch.

grav-sled. A small wheeled vehicle used for trips on the surface of a minor planet, moon, or asteroid. Not a luxurious ride.

green. When referring to a system or process, an indication that all is ready or working normally.

gripe. A malfunction or problem with a system aboard a starship.

grog. A mix of alcohol and water, beloved by starship

crewers. Also refers to alcoholic drinks imbibed in port, which shouldn't be mixed with water but often are.

gunboat. A small but heavily armed warship. Often found patrolling ports or spacelanes.

H

hail. An opening communication from one party to another.

hammock. A length of canvas or netting strung between beams belowdecks, in which crewers sleep.

hand. A crewer. Use generally limited to discussions of "all hands."

hang a leg. Do something too slowly.

hardtack. Bland starship rations that don't spoil over long cruises but aren't particularly tasty. Unlike in ancient times, hardtack is rarely actually hard.

hatchway. An opening in a ship's hull for transferring cargo to and from the hold.

head. A bathroom aboard a starship.

heading. A starship's current course.

head money. A reward for prisoners recovered.

heave to. A command for a starship to stop its motion.

heel. To lean to one side.

helm. Originally the controls for piloting a starship, but now generally a term indicating an officer is in command of a starship.

HMS. His (or Her, depending on who is the monarch) Majesty's Ship, a prefix for a warship from Earth.

hold. The area of a starship in which cargo is held. Hatchways or bay doors generally open to allow direct access to the hold.

hominy. Ground corn boiled with milk.

hoy. A small merchant coaster.

I

idler. A crewer who isn't required to keep night watches.

impression. Forced service aboard a starship during wartime.

in a clove hitch. Dealing with a dilemma.

in extremis. Unable to maneuver safely due to malfunction, damage, or some other condition. Privileged vessels must yield the right-of-way to starships in extremis.

in ordinary. Out of commission; said of a starship. Also applies to the crew of a starship while she is laid up in ordinary.

in soundings. Sufficiently close to a celestial body that its gravity must be taken into account during maneuvers.

intercept. The process of examining a starship for possible boarding, often followed by a boarding action.

interrogatories. Reports prepared about an intercept and boarding action, detailing events with evidence from the ships' records. Interrogatories are submitted as part of a claim in admiralty court.

invalid. A spacer on the sick list because of illness or injury.

J

jetsam. Objects jettisoned from a starship in distress.

job captain. A captain given temporary command of a starship while the regular captain is away or indisposed.

jolly boat. A small craft used for inspections or repairs of starships in orbit.

jump-pop. A sugary, caffeinated drink loved by children and crewers alike. Bad for you.

Jupiter Trojans. Two groups of asteroids that share an orbit with Jupiter, lying ahead of and behind the giant planet in its orbit. The group ahead of Jupiter is called the Greek node, while the trailing group is called the Trojan node. That naming convention developed after individual asteroids were named, resulting in an asteroid named after a Greek hero (617 Patroclus) residing in the Trojan camp, and an asteroid named after a Trojan hero (624 Hektor) residing in the Greek camp.

K

keel. A long girder laid down between a starship's bow and stern, giving her structural integrity.

keelhaul. To abuse someone. Derived from the ancient practice of hauling a disobedient sailor under a ship's keel.

keep the matter dark. Keep something confidential.

ketch. A short-range merchant starship.

kip. A cheap lodging house in a port.

klick. A kilometer.

L

ladderwell. A ladder connecting decks on a starship.

lagan. Cargo left behind after a shipwreck and marked by a buoy for reclamation. Lagan can be legally salvaged under certain conditions.

LaGrange point. A stable point in space where the gravitational interaction of various large bodies allows a small body to remain at rest. Space stations, roadsteads, and clumps of asteroids are often built or found at planets' LaGrange points.

landing field. An area of a port where starships land. Typically, only small starships actually use landing fields, with larger vessels remaining in orbit.

larder. A room aboard a starship in which provisions are stored.

lash up and stow. A command, typically piped, for crewers to roll up their hammocks, clearing space for shipboard operations.

launch. A small, lightly armed craft kept aboard a starship, used for short outings and errands between ships. An unarmed launch is generally called a gig.

letter of marque. A document giving a civilian starship the right to seize ships loyal to another nation, an action that otherwise would be considered piracy.

liberty. Permission to leave a ship for a time in port.

lighter. A starship used for ferrying cargo between ships and to and from ships in orbit above a port.

loblolly boy. A surgeon's assistant.

log. A record of a starship's operations.

longboat. A small starship primarily used for provisioning bigger starships.

long nine. A cannon designed to hit targets at very long range.

lumper. A laborer hired to load and unload a merchant ship in orbit or in port.

M

magazine. A section of a starship used for storing missiles and other ordnance.

marine. A soldier aboard a warship who splits his or her duties between gunnery and boarding actions. The term is typically reserved for formal military ships, though it is sometimes extended to soldiers serving for pay to defend merchant starships. Crewers who perform this role aboard civilian ships are never called marines.

mast. A pole attached to a starship's hull to maximize the capabilities of sensors and/or antennae.

master. A member of the bridge crew who is not the captain or first mate. A female crew member holding this rank is sometimes but not always called mistress.

master-at-arms. A crewer responsible for discipline belowdecks. On some ships the warrant officer or bosun serves as the master-at-arms, but wise captains avoid such an arrangement, as many crewers regard it as unfair.

matey. An affectionate word for a shipmate.

mess. Where meals are served belowdecks.

midshipman. A crewer training to be an officer. Midshipmen typically begin as children, spending years as apprentices belowdecks before being appointed to a starship's bridge crew. Low-ranking masters who are new to the bridge crew are often still called midshipmen.

moor. To secure a starship during a period of inactivity, whether in orbit or on a landing field.

musketoon. A pistol with a broad, bell-like muzzle.

"my starship." A declaration of a captain or ranking officer indicating that he or she is assuming command. Command can be assigned through the order "your starship," etc.

O

off soundings. Sufficiently far from a celestial body that its gravity can be ignored during maneuvers.

ordinary spacer. A spacer capable of performing most activities aboard a starship, but not an expert. With work, an ordinary spacer may rate as an able spacer.

ordnance. A starship's offensive weapons and materials, from cannons to missiles.

ore boat. A starship hauling ore, typically owned by a prospector.

P

packet. A small passenger boat that carries mail and personal goods between ports.

parley. A negotiation, often informal, between enemies.

parole. A prisoner's pledge of good behavior while in captivity, or conditions agreed to if released.

pass. A document indicating a starship's allegiance, and good for safe conduct from privateers aligned with a given nation. The validity of a pass is ensured by transmitting the proper recognition code.

passageway. A corridor aboard a starship.

peg. Figure, as in "I didn't peg you for a lawyer/pirate/ etc."

performance bond. A financial guarantee that a privateer will abide by the terms of its letter of marque. Fines can be levied against a performance bond by an admiralty court or by the government issuing the letter of marque.

persuader. Slang for a carbine, large knife, or other weapon that can sway the less well-armed participant in a dispute.

pinnace. A small, fast, highly maneuverable ship used for offensive and defensive operations by warships and other starships, and typically operated by either a single pilot or by a pilot and gunner.

pipe. A whistle used by the bosun to issue orders to a crew. Any spacer quickly learns to identify the unique tune for each order.

pirate. A civilian starship (or crewer aboard such a starship) that seizes or attacks other ships without authorization from a government. Piracy is punishable by death. A civilian ship with authorization for such seizures or attacks is a privateer.

pitch. A starship moving up or down through the horizontal axis. Sometimes an involuntary motion if a starship is damaged, malfunctioning, or being piloted poorly.

port. The left side of a ship, if a crewer is looking toward the bow from the stern. A starship's port hull is marked by red lights. Also, a planet, moon, or asteroid where a starship crew takes on supplies, offloads cargo, or has other business.

porthole. A small, generally round window in the hull of a starship.

press gang. A group of spacers that prowls ports, looking for men or women to impress into the navy, merchant marine, or crew of a starship. Press gangs are now rare in most ports.

privateer. A civilian starship authorized to take offensive action against another nation, typically by seizing merchant ships belonging to that nation. Unlike pirates, privateers possess a letter of marque, which requires them to abide by the laws of war and all other laws of space.

privileged vessel. A starship that has the right-of-way while navigating.

prize. An enemy vessel, crew, and cargo captured in

space by a warship or privateer. The claiming of a prize is declared legal or illegal through a hearing in admiralty court. A legally taken prize is either condemned and sold to a nation or on its behalf, or released for ransom and allowed to continue on its way. Either way, the proceeds (prize money) are divided among the ship's crew.

prize agent. An agent who sells prizes on behalf of a nation, pocketing a fee for his or her efforts.

prize court. A court that decides claims on captured starships.

prize law. The interplanetary laws governing the taking of prizes.

prize money. The proceeds from the sale of a prize and the ransom of her crew, shared out among the bridge crew and crewers at the end of a cruise.

protection. A certificate attesting that a spacer is a member of a starship's crew. Designed to thwart press gangs, though not always effective in doing so.

purser. A crewer responsible for keeping a starship's financial records and distributing provisions to crewers. Typically a role assigned by the warrant officer to a trusted veteran spacer.

put in irons. Imprison.

Q

quarterdeck. A starship's command center, often known as the bridge on civilian ships. Typically reserved for the officers of the bridge crew.

quittance. A release from a debt.

R

ransom. Money paid to pirates or privateers for the safe return of a ship and/or her crew. Also, money paid to privateers to allow a captured starship to proceed along its course without being taken to prize court for claiming and condemnation.

reactor. The power source of a starship, housed near the engines and heavily armored for protection and to prevent radiation from leaking and poisoning the crew.

recall. An order to return to a starship and prepare for liftoff.

red. In reference to a system or situation, an indication that things are not ready or functioning normally.

rescue. The recapture of a prize by a friendly ship before it can be claimed in prize court and condemned. A rescue restores the starship to its prior owners.

retainer. A crewer whose family has served aboard a starship or for a specific family or shipping company for multiple generations. Many privateers and merchants are crewed in large part by retainers.

right-of-way. An indication that a starship has priority over other starships for navigating in the area. The starship with the right-of-way is the privileged vessel; other starships are burdened vessels.

roadstead. A safe anchorage outside a port or a port's orbit, often at a space station or isolated asteroid.

roll. A starship moving to port or starboard of the horizontal axis while changing its vertical orientation. Sometimes an involuntary motion if a starship is damaged, malfunctioning, or being piloted poorly.

rudder. The device used by the pilot to steer a starship. A physical object in ancient times, but now a series of software commands.

S

salvage. To recover and legally claim abandoned or lost cargo (or a starship), or to claim subject to a legal ruling.

scope. A screen showing the result of sensor scans, or providing diagnostics about other starship functions.

scow. A dirty, poorly run starship.

scurvy. Originally a disease to which sailors were susceptible; now a term of contempt.

scuttle. To intentionally render a starship or an important system aboard a starship inoperable, so as to deny it to an enemy.

Securitat. The intelligence service of the Jovian Union.

settle one's hash. To subdue or silence someone, often violently.

shindy. A dance favored by boisterous crewers. Also: a good time had by same. A night of hijinks while at liberty in a port would be remembered as "a fine shindy."

ship of the line. A warship big and capable enough to

take part in a major battle.

shoals. The area of space near a celestial body, within which particular care must be taken by a pilot. A term borrowed from ancient sailing.

shore leave. Free time in port granted to a starship's crew.

short commons. Thin rations.

sick list. The roster of crew members ill and unable to perform their duties aboard a starship.

silent running. Operating a starship with as few systems engaged as possible in an effort to avoid detection.

slew. A maneuver by which a starship turns around on her own axis.

sloop. A small, fast starship with weapons. Sloops are smaller than corvettes and typically used for interplanetary voyages.

slop book. A register of items given to crewers by the purser. The cost of these items is subtracted from their pay or share of prize money.

soft tack. Bread or cake, a treat during long cruises.

space. As a verb, to expose someone deliberately to a vacuum, with fatal results.

spacelane. A corridor through space near a planet, moon, or asteroid, typically marked by buoys.

spike. To render a cannon inoperable.

squadron. A division of a fleet.

stand. To hold a course for a destination.

starboard. The right side of a starship, as seen from a crewer at the stern looking toward the bow. The starboard side of a starship is marked by green lights on the hull.

starship. Technically a starship is a spacegoing vessel capable of operating between planets or other distant points in space. In practice, any spacegoing vessel. Starships are called "she" and "her," with the exception of some commercial craft and small starships such as gigs, gunboats, and pinnaces. Military ships serving nations are usually called warships.

starshipwright. A designer or maker of starships.

stateroom. The cabin of a starship captain, another high-ranking officer, or an important person on board.

stern. The rear of a starship.

sternboard. A method of turning a starship when the pilot cannot maneuver forward. A real test of a pilot's ability.

stern chaser. A gun mounted at a starship's stern, used for firing at pursuing vessels.

sternpost. A thick beam rising from a starship's keel at the stern and helping to support her engines and reactor.

straggler. A crewer absent from his or her ship.

summat. Something.

supercargo. A crewer in charge of a merchant vessel's cargo. A supercargo is typically not a regular member of the crew, but a representative of the shipping line or starship's owner. Not all merchant vessels have supercargoes aboard.

surgeon. A doctor aboard a starship, whose responsibilities include treating everything from common illnesses to wounds suffered in battle. Such medical care is often rudimentary.

T

tender. A vessel that carries supplies, provisions, and personal deliveries to a warship in port.

ticket. A written document promising payment of wages or other compensation at a later date.

top deck. The uppermost deck of a starship. Often living quarters for the starship's officers, and reserved for them.

transom. The aft wall of a ship at her stern. The transom is strong and heavily reinforced, helping to support the engines and often the reactor.

transponder. An electronic system that automatically broadcasts a starship's name, operating number, home port, and nationality. Many civilian ships travel with their transponders disabled, and some broadcast false identities to confuse pirates and privateers.

tub. A slow, ungainly starship.

V

victualing yard. A part of a port where the stores of many victuallers, chandlers, and other merchants are found. Typically, purchased items are delivered later.

victualler. A starship that sells provisions to other starships in orbit above a port. Also: the owner of such a starship or his or her store in a port.

viewport. A large window in a starship, typically found on the bridge/quarterdeck.

W

wardroom. The cabin belowdecks reserved for the warrant officer and spacers assigned significant roles by him or her.

warrant officer. The ranking officer belowdecks, typically a spacer who has worked his or her way up through the ranks, but sometimes drawn from the bridge crew.

wash. The ion exhaust of a starship's engines.

watch. A period of time during which an officer, a crewer, or a group of crewers is responsible for certain operations aboard a starship. The day is divided into seven watches: the first watch lasts from 2000 to midnight, the middle watch from midnight to 0400, the morning watch from 0400 to 0800, the forenoon watch from 0800 to 1200, the afternoon watch from 1200 to 1600, the first dog watch from 1600 to 1800, and the second dog watch from 1800 to 2000.

watch officer. The ranking officer during a given watch. The watch officer retains command in the event of an emergency during his or her watch unless relieved by the captain or sometimes the first mate.

Y

yaw. A starship's motion to port or starboard of the vertical axis but maintaining the same horizontal bearing. Yaw refers only to an involuntary motion, as when a starship is damaged, malfunctioning, or being piloted poorly. A deliberate move to port or starboard of the vertical axis is simply a turn.